I0619528

NOT ANOTHER STATISTIC

A YURI SORENSON MYSTERY #1

J.M. DABNEY

Hostile
WHISPER PRESS

For the readers who follow me along the crazy path my characters decide to take them.

Special thanks to my amazing beta readers and the other people involved who keep me going no matter what.

AUTHOR'S NOTE

While this book is part of a series and has continuing main characters each book is a HFN/HEA without cliffhangers. Every book will focus on the main characters and one case with a solid resolution. The romance will continue over the course of the books.

NOT ANOTHER STATISTIC

Former Federal Agent Yuri Sorenson had left the bureau behind to become a private investigator. His ex-partner came to him asking for a favor, not knowing who else to trust. Yuri had always had a way of keeping his emotional distance from the people he protected, yet that changed the day Clarkson hesitantly limped into his life.

What happens when love is confused with pain? That's the exact question Josh Clarkson had asked himself for years. He'd grown up in an overburdened foster care system, and from what he knew of love, he couldn't expect anything but to be something tolerated. Was he meant to be more than a plaything or a piece of scenery? He could hope.

Two men who know nothing but being broken find that patience and acceptance are harder than losing hope. Is the leap of faith worth the reward of letting someone else in? Maybe they'll find the strength to find out before the danger of Josh's past tries to tear them apart.

ONE

YURI

YURI SORENSON. Private Investigator. I read the words on the door of my new office. It was as far from D.C. as I could get. At forty-five, I was burned out from the corruption around me and playing politics. I hadn't taken the job to paste on a smile and act as if everything was business as usual. That's how I ended up in a city that was just as shifty, but at least I didn't have to watch my back among friends because I didn't have any.

Galeside had just the environment for a former federal agent that wanted to get lost. And what better place to set up shop than over a strip club called Glittering Vices in the Sin District. I opened the door with my new key that I'd just picked up from the club owner, Ramone, and stepped inside to my new life. The furniture was delivered the day before, and now it was just a matter of finding some jobs.

Following cheating spouses was just fine with me. At that moment, all I cared about was paying my bills and being able to eat. The dangers of leaving before you were eligible for your pension, I was only a few years shy of my twenty-five years. No matter how I played it out in my head, I couldn't justify staying longer. The compulsion to escape made each day another to endure. I wanted nothing more than to leave that life behind and find a place to just be.

I closed the door and headed for the large, half-circle window and looked out on the neighborhood. Pimps and hookers, drug dealers and cops, and a local bar owned by the biggest crime boss in the city littered the street below. I'd chosen this place for a reason. The lowest of the low, information could always be found for a price. Everyone's money was the same color.

I'd used an old friend to run a check on all the players. You never went into a situation without knowing who you'd mix with. The door hinges squeaked behind me, and I turned, only decades of stoicism helped me hide my expression.

"What do you want?" I asked as I watched my old partner enter the office. I bent my arm behind my back and wrapped my hand around the butt of my weapon. Levi West was one of the people I wanted to put as much distance between us as possible.

"No reason to reach for that, Yuri."

"I'll reserve judgment on that, West."

"Fine, hold onto your piece, but I gotta job for you."

"No," I answered quickly. Whatever job he wanted to offer—I wasn't interested.

We stared each other down like fighters in the ring. Watching for the slightest tell that an attack was imminent. I wouldn't lie and say my paranoia was out of hand, but I'd seen too much shit the past few years to let my guard down.

"Don't answer so quickly. This is strictly off the books." He threw a file on my desk.

I removed my hand from my gun and picked up the folder. I opened it to find a picture of a boy looking back at me. Blond and too pretty, my gut said he was kept and spoiled. I didn't even have to read the file to figure that out. Twenty years as an agent and you became pretty proficient at reading people; even from a photo.

"And?"

"Josh Clarkson. Formerly affiliated with Vernon Cross."

"Why does that name sound familiar?"

"Son of Richard Cross, the Republican Senator, hoping to be president."

"Shit."

"You can say that again. Apparently, Cross likes to rough up his boyfriends, and Clarkson barely survived the beating. He's been put into protective custody for the time being, at least until after the trial. The District Attorney called us in to cut down on possible bias by local authorities. There's already been numerous threats and a few failed attempts."

"It's a rich boy with a conservative politician dad, what's that have to do with me?"

"We need to find a safehouse for him. Clarkson's not going to make it through the trial. Both Crosses have the boy on their hitlist. Which means he's gonna end up being found floating in the harbor or in an alley execution-style."

I threw the file back in his direction. This shit was why I quit. I had no interest in babysitting some brat and just having the kid end up dead anyway. Sex and politics were a recipe for being six-feet-under. Throw in a homophobic, politician father wanting to lessen embarrassment, and I might as well kiss my ass goodbye.

"It seems you're in need of a job, and Clarkson needs a bodyguard."

"Fuck, no. You're not pulling me back just to have someone shoot at my hairy ass over a domestic dispute."

"You're the only one I got to ask, Yuri. This kid isn't going to make it through this trial. There's already been three attempts. We don't know if it's the Senator or the son, or both."

I growled as I picked up the file and started going through it. Kid was in his mid-twenties. "How long has Cross been keeping him?"

"Complete isolation for a year, together I think two or three years. Seems Cross sweet-talked Josh. Found out the kid aged out of the system. Has a history of abusive boyfriends. Perfect target for someone who just wants an ass to fuck and can do whatever they want to him."

"When does the trial start?" My paranoia flared to life, and I mentally tallied all the ways an operation like this could go wrong.

"Two days."

"Nice way to wait until the last minute."

"We got word that his last protection detail was compromised. We needed to step outside official channels on this one."

I flipped more pages, and Clarkson's entire life was in the file. Even petty shoplifting charges, vagrancy, and some alleged solicitation. But he'd never gone in front of a judge for the prostitution. I scanned the psychological evaluation that the defense had asked the prosecution to perform.

"And I'm the lucky one?"

"No one cleaner than you."

I wasn't sure about that. I'd left before the guilty-by-association verdict came down from my superiors. "What's in it for me?"

"Double your daily rate plus expenses until the end of the trail. Or would you rather follow around a cheating wife or find someone's lost dog?"

I hated that I was motivated by money, but I had bills to pay. I laid the file back on my empty desk and pretended to think it over. Just because West had me by the balls didn't mean I couldn't make him sweat a bit.

"When do I meet him?"

"He's outside the door."

I groaned and thought about pulling my weapon, but a former federal agent didn't stand a chance in prison. He stuck his hand into his jacket and pulled out an envelope. When he held it out to me, I ripped it from his grip.

"That has cash, hotel address and card keys, also when to be at the courthouse. I'll be your handler on this. You don't contact anyone else, and as of this minute, I'm the only one who knows he's with you."

He turned and opened the door, leaning out and then a dangerously thin young man entered my office. His face was covered with small scars as if someone had taken a razor to him. His full bottom lip was marred by a thick scar that split the center of the curve. His gait was slightly uneven as if favoring his hip.

"Josh, this is Yuri Sorenson, he's going to be taking care of you until the trial is over with."

"Hello, Mr. Sorenson." His voice was soft and timid.

I wasn't surprised. His file gave me insight that the kid was beaten down by life and just about every man he'd bent over for. I should be more sympathetic. This wasn't my first protection duty. My superiors had assigned me to every witness security detail that came across their desks.

"I'll leave you two to get acquainted. Yuri, you have my number."

Fuck, West left like his ass was on fire and I studied the kid, and the way he looked everywhere but at me. I closed his file and tucked the envelope inside.

"Tell me you got a bag."

"Yes, it's in the hall."

"Not the safest place to leave your things, kid." I didn't miss the kid's flinch. "Come on, good thing I hadn't unpacked my vehicle yet. Let's get to the hotel and get you locked down for the night."

I figured tonight would be the safest to get him to a room and then I could walk the layout of the hotel for escape routes and weak spots in security. I'd have to get employee records and IDs, especially for room service. It would be safer for me to pick up from the hotel restaurant. I shook my head and pushed off the unknown variables for the time being. Enough opportunity to think about it later when I had the kid in a room, and I could get a minute to think.

"Grab your bag," I ordered, and even though I tried to soften my tone, it still came out harsher than I intended. The kid was beaten down, you could see it in the way he carried himself, and I didn't understand why it was pissing me off the way it did. I didn't need some emotionally scarred boy with masochistic tendencies pushing my damn buttons.

Instead of going out front, I led him to the fire exit at the back, and down the alley. I shoved him behind me as we came to the corner. I pulled my weapon and kept it at my side as I checked the surroundings.

"Put your hood up and stay behind me." Thankfully, he listened, and I grabbed his hand, keeping him close. My car was at the end of the block, and as long as West covered his tail on the way to my office, we should be good. I kept a hold of the kid's hand, and when we reached my SUV, I got him in the front seat and his bag in the back. Everything I owned was in there, which wasn't much. I'd learned to travel light from my teens. No reason for permanence when I knew nothing lasted forever.

As quickly as possible, I had us headed across the city to the high-priced hotel. I would've been happier with a no-tell-motel where the employees didn't ask too many questions. If the hotel didn't pan out, maybe that would be our next location. First rule was always to have a backup plan.

I scrubbed my hand over my face. So much for a nice quiet retirement. All I could hope was I didn't end up dead.

TWO

JOSH

GLOSSY IMAGES WERE DISPLAYED under the glare of the courtroom lights. My eyelids twitched as I studied the visual documentary of my life. It was fingertip bruises on my pale skin that was stretched over my starved muscles. Swollen eyelids mottled in varying shades of black, purple and yellow—old and new bleeding wide over the battered canvas that was my body. An evenly modulated voice rose and fell at just the right moment for emphasis and effect as the attorney narrated—my twenty-five years morphed into no more than a docket number.

My eyes fell on yet another piece of evidence pointed out to the jury members. My tongue stroked the thickly scarred curve of my bottom lip. I was a victim, born and bred. It was only right the end of my so-called perfect life with Vernon Cross would come down to this moment. Stiffly sitting on a hard, dark-stained bench behind the prosecutor's table and listening to my every shame highlighted for strangers.

I was one large aching muscle and festering wound. I turned into a statistic for emphasis in a PSA—some afterschool special. The aftereffect of balled fists pounding into mere mortal flesh, a nauseating symphony of sledgehammer punches which never seemed to end.

How did I come to be here? Born, abandoned, and possibly starved for love of any kind. Was this moment predestined: A fate foretold? I drowned out the drone of voices, the heaviness of my ex's murderous glare and did it all with ease.

I found my mythical happy place—all sunny skies and unfettered happiness. Was it only months before that I could've been any face in the crowd? I was just another stranger blending into the scenery, seen in some surreal peripheral aspect and just as easily forgotten.

Yet, now the spotlight brightly shined down on my blond hair. The attention was blinding and uncomfortable in its intensity. My brain screamed—pled—for me to flee, but my body was frozen in place. I lived the highlighted memories in white-hot, painful clarity. The refresher course of a trial wasn't needed to make me remember it was all there as soon as I closed my eyes.

I was simply hoping for an end to the day's festivities of rehashing the facts ad nauseam.

My ex was a multi-millionaire CEO and conservative senator's son, those made this a high-profile case. My doubts that he would get more than a slap on the wrist or the fact I would even survive until the end grew exponentially.

The embarrassment of an attempted murder trial wouldn't go unpunished. He rather enthusiastically enjoyed his lessons. My fingertips trailed over the bandage securing the cracked ribs from my last lesson. I was essentially a no one in the great scheme of things. An unwanted child birthed by an uninterested mother, then later by an overburdened foster care system after she'd attempted to drown me.

I shook my head as I tightly wrapped my arms around myself. The twinge of pain in my ribs pulled me back to the present. I sensed I was being watched as the hairs rose on the back of my neck.

Protective custody, that's what they'd called it. I refused to glance back to check if my shadow still held fast to his post. The unnerving prickly sensation assured him he was there.

To anyone else Yuri Sorenson would appear as if he were just a casual observer. I'd vehemently protested the need for the large, intimidating presence of Sorenson when Agent West had called to check in the day before. Part of me felt there was more to it than they told me—more than just an attempted murder and a rich man wanting to get off with probation at worse. Plenty of questions demanded answers, but as the saying goes: beware what you ask for. I had enough trouble—I wasn't going to borrow more.

My head was fucked-up and mired in reality-bending flashbacks. The slightest movements or loud voices caused me to flinch and cower. I'd lived with the fear for so long that it was simply second nature. The first hit of my life came at the age of six. I don't remember what I'd done or even if I'd done anything, yet the hit came all the same.

More often than not, I expected the abuse—affection and gentleness were foreign concepts. I accepted the flashes of pain rather than the warm softness of love. My too loud sigh pierced the near silence of the courtroom as the judge called a recess for the day. Opening arguments were complete, the formalities waning to make way for the actual trial. Everyone stood as the judge pushed to his feet. The judge's chair creaked beneath his shifting weight, and then he exited.

The bailiff stood tall at his post at the front of the room. The large man's shoulders were squared, right hand wrapped around his left wrist and his booted feet a shoulder-width apart. He stood beside the witness stand.

The knowledge that one day soon I'd have to sit in the

witness seat made bile burn bitter at the back of my throat. I'd told the story so many times, knew each detail by heart, but Vernon's lawyers could and possibly would tear me apart.

Would my past come into play? The few lovers the defense could find possibly paraded in front of the jury—the lovers who came close to doing exactly what Vernon had.

I waited for the courtroom to clear and intently listened as I tried to ignore Vernon and his team of lawyers as they left. Jurors mumbled beneath their breaths in low drones. Words blended in an annoying humming. The door hinges in dire need of oiling creaked as they opened and closed. The click of heels or the heaviness of boots echoed off the walls, and sneakers squeaked on slick, tile floors.

"Mr. Clarkson."

A hoarse, deep voice called my name. I turned my head to find Sorenson watching me with an odd look in his hazel eyes. If I didn't know better, I'd almost believe it was concern. That emotion was too soft for the hard, taciturn man.

"Yes?" I asked. Sorenson refused to use my first name. I assumed it was to keep some distance between himself and me. To him, I wasn't anything other than a job. A way to earn a paycheck.

"Mr. Cross has left. It's time for us to head back to the hotel."

I only nodded. It's not as if I could protest and tell Sorenson to take me home. Home for the last three years was Vernon's penthouse. He hadn't allowed me to keep a job either. I was stupid in my romantic notions of Vernon loving and wanting to take care of me. We'd even talked marriage a few times. I'd seen through the pretense for what it was. A proposal would be like any gift given as an apology for my treatment. Candy to shut the kid up.

"Mr. Clarkson, we need to go."

The order was unmistakable in Sorenson's voice. In our short acquaintance, I'd learned he didn't like to repeat himself. He expected immediate compliance with his orders, and you never questioned said instructions. As was my nature, I never inquired merely followed.

I straightened to my full height of barely an even six-foot. I learned during my post-attempted murder physical that I was thirty pounds underweight. A skeleton existed beneath the cheap suit I wore, protruding bony hips, ribs, and the knobby line of my spine.

Sorenson walked a few steps behind me, far enough to remain inconspicuous, yet close enough to avert possible disaster.

How the wall of angry looking muscle could pretend to be unobtrusive, I hadn't a clue. Maybe it was the fact he wasn't pretty or even conventionally handsome that made him unremarkable. To be honest, I thought most would find his face too weathered and grim to be even remotely attractive.

All I knew was I wasn't looking forward to another night of stony silence. He was a man of practically no words. If a conversation had the potential for friendliness, my watchdog would excuse himself for the night. Not to say I'm all that chatty, to begin with. If it was up to me, I'd go days without speaking, but the silence trapped me within my thoughts. The remembering—the flashbacks—was too much to handle.

As I'd expected, the ride back to the hotel they'd put me up in was made in silence. He checked the rearview and the side mirrors. I thought about starting a round of idle chitchat. Turning on the radio was a no-no, he didn't seem interested in TV, music or anything else that would potentially take his focus away from the job. Shortly I'd be asked what I wanted for dinner—I'd answer and receive a grunt in reply.

I'd never made friends easily or at all really. I was the quintessential loner archetype. That old cliché if someone looked up antisocial in the dictionary there'd be a nice little picture of me. I darted a glance toward him and caught the jumping of his jaw muscle beneath his trimmed salt and pepper beard. He seemed irritated, but I figured that was normal for him. If he ever smiled, his face would probably shatter. I sighed before I could stop myself.

"Problem?" he asked.

The question surprised me. It took a few tries to get an answer out. "No," I nearly stuttered.

"Okay."

The word was spoken with finality as if his tone alone would end any conversation that may occur, and I couldn't let it go at that.

"Do you have a problem with me?" I asked as I turned my head to watch him. He never took his eyes off the busy street or the regular checks of the mirrors.

"No." The monosyllable answer annoyed me.

Part of me wanted to cower as I'd always done, but another wanted to start an argument. I was in foreign territory, and as painful as my comfort zone was, it was the only one I knew. The pain of a punch or slap would bring me back to reality, and I would find my even footing again.

"You're lying," I accused, and for the first time, hazel eyes flaring with anger turned my way. I held my breath, I steeled myself for it and waited—and waited.

"Listen, kid, I don't give a fuck if you think I'm lying or not."

"You did it again."

"Do you have some twisted need to be popped in the mouth? Would it make you feel better?"

My face flamed as he called me on my motive.

"Even if you were up to fighting weight, I still outweigh you by over a hundred pounds. You might like to fuck assholes who love to use you as a punching bag, but you're not using me to get your rocks off. We clear?"

I didn't answer—just turned to stare out the passenger side window. Was that what it was? Did I need to be hurt to feel loved or normal? Looking back on my short life, I realized every whispered loving word was confessed after a beating or punishing sex. When did natural and loving become associated with physical and emotional pain? I lapsed into silence and drew my mind away from any more soul searching. I'd pushed my luck with him—a man I didn't think had a forgiving nature.

THREE

YURI

I RETURNED to the room after doing a quick walkthrough and checking the exits. The kid barely made it into the room before he'd crashed. I'd watched him throughout the opening arguments, and he took it like a physical blow. There wasn't much I hadn't seen in my life, but the sheer amount of abuse he'd suffered made even me flinch. I was amazed the kid survived the beating he had, especially with the extent of his malnourishment.

I crossed the room. "What do you want for dinner?" I asked. I avoided glancing at the delicate man on the couch with his slender hands folded on his lap.

The conversation I'd avoided earlier still played in my mind.

The provocation wasn't expected, and nothing surprised me anymore. I'd worked protection detail most of my former career. It was an aspect of the job I loved and hated. I hated this particular assignment. The silence stretched, and I roughly sighed as I turned to look at Josh.

Josh Clarkson was pretty in a fragile way. I felt sympathy, but something about the kid put me on edge. A broken feeling emanated in overwhelming waves from his emaciated body, and an uneasy prickle traveled beneath my skin. He was giving up, and there was no one who'd stop him from continuing to self-destruct.

"Kid, did you hear me?" I wasn't completely heartless, or at least I hoped.

Round blue eyes met mine before glancing away, "A small salad." It was the only answer I received, and it wasn't satisfactory.

"You're eating more than that." I picked up the phone, called a local place to order burgers and fries, a chocolate milkshake for the kid. I wasn't taking no for an answer. Yet, he didn't protest. He didn't have any fight left in him, and maybe he never did.

Hanging up, I moved across the room and took a seat in front of the picture window. The drawn curtains blocked out anyone who might get too nosy.

I'd studied the kid's file, and as much as I'd wanted to turn down the job, something stopped me. It wasn't that I couldn't turn down a job protecting an abuse victim. I was an imposing scary man, I'd always been oversized, and it worked well for my career. My past also played a big part in why I'd taken the cases no one else wanted.

I grew up with a single mother. My drunken father showed up only long enough to use my mother and leave her with bruises to remember him by. Normally, I had an easier touch with the victims of domestic violence, although, the kid's demeanor put me on edge. Straight, white teeth worried the curve of his full bottom lip. I'd noticed he only did it when he was nervous, which meant most of the time. He focused mostly on the thick scar bisecting his lower lip.

The urge to place my fingers under Josh's pointed chin and force his eyes upward strengthened. I'd spent too many years observing my mother staring into space or down at her feet. I hadn't been able to save her, and the guilt still ate at me. Conditioned over decades of abuse, she'd never broken away from my father. At the age of sixteen, I'd come home to find she'd taken her last beating.

As always, a lump formed in my throat and threatened to choke me. I still remembered her blood-streaked face and wide eyes that had sightlessly watched me. She'd been positioned perfectly so that she'd been the first thing I saw when I'd opened the door. I'd spent years afterward plotting my revenge for when he was released from prison. Shifting my hulking frame in the uncomfortable chair, I pushed the memories away. It was in the past, and after serving just three years, my father died. That was twenty-six years ago, and the memories were just as clear as the day I'd walked into my childhood home for the last time to pack a single bag before going to the group home.

My brow furrowed as I caught him peeking at me occasionally. "You have something on your mind?" I shouldn't have asked. I was already walking a dangerous line when it came to the younger man. I wasn't anywhere near the closet, yet I didn't advertise. I couldn't deny I found the kid attractive. Josh wasn't my type though. And even if he was, it would be inappropriate. He hit all my trigger points, submissive being one of the biggest and that side of him wasn't fostered in a healthy way. He was a masochist, and I wasn't one to dole out pain or punishment only for the hell of it. Punishment was for correction of bad behavior only, anything other than that was abusive and abhorrent to me.

"So you think I asked for it?" he asked.

I didn't have to ask what, I already knew. "No, I don't think you asked for it."

"But you said..." he paused.

A sigh slipped past his full lips, and I felt like an ass. I was always an asshole. It was a major personality flaw, but a Neanderthal bastard wasn't fucked with a lot. It made people keep their distance from me.

Any attachment wasn't an option in my job. They were just files and numbers, sometimes aliases. I grabbed that day's paper and settled in to read until dinner arrived. I opened the front section of the paper with a loud snap. The sharp sound caused him to flinch, and I hated the moment of remorse that urged me to soothe him.

I was careful with sudden movements or the distance I kept. As a man my size and in this line of work, I was hyperaware of my overwhelming presence—especially when it came to abuse survivors.

"You don't like me, do you?"

I folded the paper carefully and set it aside with deliberately slow motions.

I compressed my back teeth. A growl threatened to rumble up and out of my chest. "I don't have to like you. You're a job—not my friend—kid." Why couldn't I be nice to the kid? Something about him made it impossible for me to show civility.

"Oh, okay, is it just me?"

"What's the question you really want to ask? Quit fucking pussy-footing around it. I'm not known for my patience."

"If you don't like me, how are you going to protect me?"

"Liking isn't a requirement, kid. I've protected criminals and victims alike. It's just my job. I don't have to like it or the people I keep an eye on."

Thankfully a knock came and cut off any more questions the kid would ask. I straightened to my full height and placed my hand on my sidearm—my thumb releasing the safety. Slightly lowering my head, I checked the peephole.

I observed the male on the other side of the door. No darting gaze or nervous shifting, I didn't want to order room service until West sent me over the employee records. Still cautious, I kept my fingers wrapped around the familiar grip of my gun. It fit perfectly in the cup of my palm as I soundlessly pulled it from my holster. The familiar weight of my weapon against my thigh calmed me as I cracked the door open. I checked the hallway to make sure no one was hiding at either end. I holstered my weapon, reached into my pocket to take out enough to cover the food and tip. I took the bags along with to-go cups and then slammed and locked the door.

I mentally cursed as he came off the couch. "Time to eat."

He crossed the room, and I handed him his food and milk-shake plus a bottle of water. He stood there staring at the container in his hands as if he didn't know what it was.

"Go sit down," I ordered. Josh instantly obeyed, but if shit went nuclear, I couldn't yell out for him to move every time. Tomorrow after court, we'd have to go over procedures in the event that we had to vacate the room. Where to go and wait for me—a few self-defense moves. All I could hope was he didn't freeze and that his instincts for survival kicked in.

Maybe I should've said no and let someone else take the assignment. No, that wouldn't have worked either. I understood the kid. I knew the damage abuse could do and how it skewed your perceptions, but that didn't mean I was any less frustrated with what I had to do.

As was my usual M.O., I stood at the counter and ate my dinner but kept a close eye on him to make sure he ate everything I ordered for him. Fatty foods weren't the healthiest way to put back on the pounds, but at least it was more than some tiny salad. The pictures I'd seen before the police ones showed a boy with rounded cheeks and not gaunt ones that sunk in until he was nearly skin on a skeleton. If I thought he was naturally thin, I wouldn't be so worried. Fuck, I shouldn't care at all. I just needed to keep him alive until sentencing, and they'd probably put him in witness protection.

I'd do my job. I didn't have to develop a soft spot for the kid. At twenty-five, he was old enough to take care of himself. With some counseling, he might even live a normal life one day. I just had to make sure he made it to that point.

He was eating slow, pinching off tiny bites, even breaking his fries apart. Each bite carefully chewed and swallowed, followed by a small sip of his shake. He seemed to be struggling, and I kept my mouth shut. He'd stop when he was full, and he could eat the rest later.

All I wanted to do was lay down. I was exhausted and irritated. My body was feeling every one of its years and then some. I had plans to make before I could sleep and wished I'd turned down this damn case.

FOUR

JOSH

DAY three of the trial had ended, and I was emotionally and mentally exhausted. I was ready for it to be over; I didn't care if I died, at least that way I wouldn't have to worry about anyone trying to kill me. I stepped out of the shower and started to dry off.

Knuckles loudly rapped on the door, and I jumped, barely keeping in a scream. My heart was beating so fast that my head felt light.

"Kid, you have a visitor, hurry up."

I held onto the counter and swiped a hand towel across the fogged surface. I tried not to look at myself too much. Every pink scar was a phantom pain as I remembered the slice of the knife or the strike of Vernon's fists. The tang of my own blood filled my mouth as he'd loosened teeth and split my lip.

A part of me wanted it. Pain was all I knew. He'd used me brutally, and I'd never said no. The pain and degradation were familiar and comfortable. Maybe I did ask for it. Maybe I was too sick and broken to accept anything else. Abuse was better than no touch at all. Instead of causing harm to myself, I'd found others to do it—different men but all the same.

I felt I was running out of time, and I didn't want him beating on the door again. I dried off and put on my t-shirt and sleep pants, brushed my teeth, and combed my hair. Before I left the bathroom, I cleaned everything up and folded the towels because he liked to take his shower at night. I didn't want to leave a mess for him.

I drew air into my lungs through my nose and exhaled to the count of six, repeated it until I felt centered; as centered as I could ever get. I opened the door and stepped out to find Agent West and Yuri facing off. The tension was almost suffocating as if I walked into a force field. I'd sensed that first night West introduced me to Yuri that they weren't friends, but this felt like something else—a hatred maybe.

"Josh, so glad to see Sorenson seems to be treating you well."

"He's been very professional, Agent West." I cast a glance at him to find the big man glaring at me, and I couldn't help drawing physically inward in an attempt to make myself a smaller target.

"Wouldn't expect anything else. He was always the best at his job. The prosecutor wanted to make sure you were ready for your testimony tomorrow."

"As ready as I can be."

"Well, come sit down, and we'll go over a few things to make sure you're ready."

A tremor started at my toes and worked upward as I struggled to make it to the chair West motioned to. Yuri backed up until he pressed his shoulder to the wall beside where the floor to ceiling glass started. The curtains had stayed closed as he said it was dangerous. Someone could get a shot at me from another building. I wanted to question him about why a sniper would want to take me out. I was unimportant. Whatever testimony I gave would be refuted by the witnesses—the many men I was sure they'd call.

"Josh, sit." The command in Yuri's gruff voice had me running to the chair, and I sat down.

My arms circled my body, and I rocked in what my psychiatrist from my teen years called self-soothing. They said it was an effect from being denied touch and affection, skin-starved from the time I was a baby.

"Tell me what happened that night." West didn't even ask— it was an order.

I glanced over at Yuri, and he nodded. At his command, I turned back to the agent.

"Vernon came home late from work, and he was mad about something, then he didn't like the dinner I made." I could feel the nausea building. A bottle of water entered my line of vision, and I took it, thanking Yuri and only getting a grunt in answer. His presence quickly disappeared, and I swore I felt it almost like a physical withdrawal.

"And...what happened after dinner?"

"He didn't eat. He took a bite and spit it onto the plate. I waited for the hit that always came when I didn't do something right." All their attention was on me, I felt it like a burning sensation on my nape, and I wanted to scream for them to stop. To shout no and not have to answer questions. I didn't want to relive that night. *Just say it and get it over with,* I ordered myself, but it wasn't working. I wasn't brave or strong. I was just me. "He hit me. Backhand first, then when the chair tipped back with me in it, he was on me. And he hit and hit, and I screamed for help, but no one came. Not even Vernon's security. They just let it happen. For days he locked me in my room..."

"Your room?"

I looked at West, and I hated him. I was enraged he wanted to rip open wounds that barely healed. "We had separate rooms. He only came in when he wanted to use me. For days he beat me, took a razor to me, he'd only wait until I stopped crying before he'd start again."

"What else did he do?"

"He fucked me, is that what you want to hear? No lube. No prep. Just fucked me while he pushed my face into a pillow." I was practically screaming and choking back sobs before I finished the last word.

"West, that's enough, he'll be ready for tomorrow. It's time for you to go."

Yuri's booming voice came from too close, and I couldn't help curling into a ball in the chair. Then all I could see was his back blocking out my tormentor. Protecting me as was his job.

"If he even stutters tomorrow, we're fucked putting this asshole behind bars."

"Completely destroying him before he testifies isn't going to help your cause."

"There's three men ready to testify that he liked gang bangs and being beaten during sex. They say this isn't the first time he liked a little cutting while taking it up his—"

"Get the fuck out."

I was out of the chair and hiding behind it as Yuri walked West out. He was holding the agent's jacket and belt, and then the door was slamming.

"Josh, come out." His voice wasn't any softer, but I couldn't disobey. When I stood every muscle in my body shook so badly that I barely stayed on my feet. I swiped at the tears with trembling hands and sniffled as snot touched my top lip.

"You're going to go wash your face and go to bed, do you understand me?"

"Ye-yes, sir."

He didn't move away from the door, and I was relieved that he didn't come near me. I was a raw, open wound, exposed nerves being abraded. And I rushed to the bathroom and didn't linger as I quickly washed my face and headed to the single bedroom of the suite. I didn't pull down the sheets, I laid on top and curled into a fetal position. I hugged my legs to my chest, and now that I was alone, I let the tears go. I didn't censor my loud sobs. He was in the living room, and I was just a job.

He didn't care that months—years—of pain and humiliation all came to the surface. It wasn't the first time that I'd told the story, but the strong, put-together man hadn't been there to hear it. He already had such a low opinion of me. He didn't like me. He believed I asked for it and I was too fucked-up not to disagree. I was an unworthy thing. A mistake. A failed abortion. Everything about me was wrong, and there was nothing I could do about it; I wasn't even brave enough to slit my own wrists. I'd swallowed a bottle of sleeping pills the first night in custody and woke up in a pool of vomit, and still very much in pain.

I couldn't go on like this anymore. What did I have left? After the trial, I'd be on the streets. No job or place to live, I'd be homeless again, my only home was any shelter with an open cot and a soup kitchen to have at least one meal. I'd done it before. But when Vernon had taken me off the streets, showered me with gifts and gave me a place to live—he cruelly gave me something to hope for. No job, no address, no address, no job, it was an endless cycle, and while I had a place to call for emergency help, I didn't want to go back there.

Just like with everywhere else, I wondered if I'd be welcomed. It was the only place I'd felt safe and wanted, maybe not how I craved, but it had been a safe space. I closed my eyes and forced myself to sleep. In twelve hours, I'd have to arrive at the courthouse and lay it all out, and Yuri wouldn't be there to stand between me and Vernon.

FIVE

YURI

THE KID WAS ALMOST DONE—THREE hours of testimony and every objection from the prosecution was overruled. The longer it went on, the duller his eyes became. My jaw clenched, and my back teeth ground together. There wasn't any chance Cross was going to earn a guilty plea. I'd studied the jurors. I could see the disgust as they watched the kid. Every question the defense attorney asked was more disgusting than the one before.

Each innocent answer distorted into something else. And it wasn't right—nothing was right about this trial. It was a media circus. They might as well shut this bullshit down and just let Cross walk the fuck out a free man. If the kid wasn't broken before, he sure as hell was now.

I clenched my fists behind my back, and just as I was about to cause a distraction, the judge called for a recess until the next day at nine a.m., and I strode toward him just as he was about to collapse. The stares caused the hair on the back of my neck to stand up. Something told me that we'd need to move on to another safehouse. First, I needed to get him back to our room. I escorted him out, and we made it to my vehicle. I pulled out my key fob, pushed the remote start as a precaution.

He still hadn't said a word, and I had to take his slight weight as he leaned against my side. As I scooped him into my arms, he twisted his hands in my suit jacket.

The urge to soothe him came to the surface, but I pushed it down. Instead, I got him settled on the passenger seat and buckled him in. I glanced at his face. He wasn't there. His eyes were dead, and his pale face was a sickly ashen color. I slammed the door and jogged around to the driver's side. I opened the door and slid into the driver's seat.

My curiosity had gotten the better of me, and I'd studied the case files, read more about his history. The kid didn't know what a healthy relationship was, and my sympathy had grown. As I had gone over his medical files, my experience told me the kid shouldn't be alive. Malnutrition, broken bones, blood loss, and countless other wounds should have killed him.

I pushed it all aside until I had him back to the hotel and settled, ordered him into a bath, then he needed food and caffeine. And a night's rest. After court tomorrow we'd move on to a place I was more comfortable protecting him. Someplace West and no one else would know about.

THREE HOURS LATER, I had him out of the bath, dressed and wrapped in a blanket on the couch. I'd kept my distance. The way he flinched was a huge flashing neon sign to stay away. I'd ordered food, something light that wouldn't upset his stomach after the stress of the day. I stood in the kitchenette area and stared at his profile. He stared off into space at nothing. He didn't fight or flee. He simply waited for the next hit or order to do whatever some man wanted him to.

His submissiveness enticed me. I let myself release the reins on my thoughts. His inherent shyness said he needed structure and a firm hand, but that wouldn't be me. He was a job, but that didn't mean my urges weren't pushing at my control.

The knock at the door distracted me. I strode to the door, looked through the peephole, and saw an employee I recognized from the files. Whether I recognized him or not, I drew my weapon and opened the door.

"ID?" I asked as the muzzle of a gun came into view. I slammed the door shut and turned to a wide-eyed Josh.

I darted across the room, wrapped my arm around the kid's thin waist, and hauled him off the couch. Instinct kicked in, and my exit plan played out in my head as I headed for the connecting door that led to the next room. I kicked it open before jerking him in front of me. Shots rang out, and a door banged against the wall in our room. He was thankfully quiet as I opened the door to check the hallway.

The kid was leaning against the wall beside the door as I peeked out. With my weapon held firmly in my hands, I checked each end of the hallway. "Move to your left and hug the wall, now," I ordered, and he bolted around me.

Something felt off about the attempt, but I didn't have time to think about it now. I needed to get him to a second secure location. Where...I didn't have any idea. No one should've known where we were. According to West very few knew he was in protective custody. Yes, I'd rushed forward in court, but I'd done everything to make sure we weren't followed, even taking the long way around the city. I shoved the thoughts away as I focused only on our safety and that was getting him out of there breathing.

The fire exit came up on the left, and I reached out to wrap my fist in his thin shirt.

The kid was already panting for breath, but my admiration

for the kid grew as Josh didn't complain or question. Fire tore through my right shoulder and upper chest twice. I cursed as the pain forced me to drop my gun hand. Even through the pain, I reached for him putting myself between the kid and danger and leaned us both down to grab my gun.

Shouts and heavy steps echoed off the walls of the stairway. At least a five-man team was pursuing us, and these weren't just thugs looking for a quick payday. They had some training. The agony of the gunshots dimmed my vision at the corners, yet I pushed through it, exchanging fire with our pursuers until the kid pushed open the door to the underground garage.

I grabbed my keys and hit the remote start. "You have to drive." His only reply was a tiny nod as we quickly reached my vehicle. My steps faltered as I ran around the front of it. I got in the passenger seat as fast as possible.

Having him drive wasn't the brightest idea, but neither was me passing out and killing us to finish the job of the gunmen. Where we were headed, I wasn't sure. Fuck, I needed a doctor, but it wasn't safe. I hadn't had time to scope out a possible vet or doctor that would take a bribe for a patch job.

I flinched as he pulled out of the parking spot with a lurch. Okay, having the kid drive was an even worse idea than I'd previously thought. My head fell back onto the headrest, and I forced it upward. I needed to stay conscious. I repeated the order in my head, but my body was quickly giving up to blood loss and pain. We weren't going to make it.

"Sorenson, where—"

His voice faded out, and the pressure I applied to my wounds wasn't helping when I felt the blood pumping just as quickly down my back. I wasn't going to last, and I did the one thing I shouldn't have, I let my eyes close and hoped the former street kid could come up with a plan to make it out.

SIX

JOSH

MY FINGERS WERE white from the death grip on the steering wheel. "Sorenson?" I frantically called his name, yet the only response I received was pain-filled grunts. What the hell was I supposed to do? *Think, Josh, think!* I silently ordered myself as I checked the mirrors. I didn't even know what I was supposed to be looking for. I'd seen him glancing from mirror to mirror, but would I even recognize if someone was behind us?

A fear-induced adrenaline overload raced through my veins, and I shook as I carefully weaved through traffic. I glanced at him. Red stained the white t-shirt from shoulder to waist. He needed a doctor. He was going to kill me. I checked the street signs and took the next left. I didn't have any choice—it was either call in some old friends or let him die, I couldn't do that.

There was only one person and place I knew that would be safe, but they wouldn't appreciate a former cop or federal agent being brought to their doorstep. I tried to think of other options, but there weren't any. I drove toward the city limits, and an old service station I knew had an old payphone that still worked.

The street kids had an underground, and when someone needed medicine, food, a place to stay or medical attention, or whatever, they knew who to call with no questions asked. Sorenson was losing too much blood, and it was probably already too late, but I had to try.

Fifteen minutes later, I pulled into the empty station. Lights shined inside, but I knew the attendant was asleep. Wasn't much else to do out this way and most likely the same old man worked there.

I kept the SUV running as I found enough change and jumped out of the car. My fingers were shaking so badly that I fumbled with the phone and almost misdialed the number. I took a few calming breaths and tried again.

"What?" The cranky voice that answered almost had me smiling.

"In the cold." I used the old code.

"Fifteen minutes, don't be late."

It was the only reply before the line went dead. The pickup point would be a park and ride not far away. I hurried back to the vehicle because fifteen minutes meant fifteen. I hopped in. The safehouse wasn't far, and luckily, I spotted no other vehicles on my way. The old road ran parallel to the highway, and it didn't get much traffic. I pulled into the empty park and ride; a van waited with its headlights on.

We'd have to leave the vehicle. Not everything was on the up and up with the underground. I pulled to a stop and quickly searched him for anything else that would show he had anything to do with law enforcement. The gun had to go, as well. I took it from Sorenson's limp fingers and quickly locked it in the glove compartment and shoved his wallet into the pocket of my jeans.

"We ain't got all day."

I jumped at the voice coming through the open driver's side window.

"I need help. I can't move him by myself."

"Fuck."

The once annoyed voice changed at the sound of my voice. I couldn't believe Frank was still working for Arianna.

"We need help over here."

They muscled Sorenson out of the car—which wasn't easy with his size. Him not fighting them concerned me even more. I sat on the floor in the back of the dark van with his head on my lap.

"What the fuck happened, Josh?" Frank asked.

"My ex sent some guys after me...he got hurt protecting me. I didn't know who else to call."

"We saw on the news. You were always shit when picking boyfriends."

"I don't need to hear it." We lapsed into silence as I placed my hand over the holes in Sorenson's shoulder. The blood was warm as it oozed between my fingers. His face was pale, and I felt for his pulse, but I couldn't feel it. But he was breathing even though it was just shallow.

"Does he have anything on him?"

"No, I checked his pockets. He doesn't have a phone or anything else." I knew the routine. Paranoia was second nature, and it was worse when it came to cops. They'd been fucked over so many times they trusted almost no one. If they found out Sorenson was a former agent, I would quickly make the long list of people not to trust. This was the only place I'd felt safe or as if I belonged. My past stays were short; sometimes, a few months at the most. Yet, I remembered I could breathe.

On the drive, my mind flashed back to the events before all hell broke loose. He put himself between me and the gunmen. Got himself shot to protect me. I nervously chewed my bottom lip. The big man couldn't die.

An old metal gate squeaking as it opened broke into my thoughts. The sound was familiar. I'd heard it enough on the nights I'd called Arianna for help. Everything happened in hyper-speed as chaos descended and he was carried into the old non-descript mansion. The property and house had been abandoned decades ago and bought to act as a safe haven and sometimes a brief stop on the way to freedom. Arianna's pale silver hair shimmered under the porch lights.

"Josh." Arianna's tone was quiet and concerned. Thin yet strong arms wrapped around me. "Let's get you inside."

"I have to go with him."

Arianna shook her head to cut me off. She might look like the maternal type, but she wasn't one to allow her orders to be disobeyed. It reminded me of Sorenson.

"There isn't anything you can do for him. Doc's got him covered. How the hell did you get even skinnier, boy? You never had the greatest taste in men."

"I've heard that before."

I was aware I had bad taste in men. I wanted to be loved and needed; I took it however I could get it even if it came with broken bones and fingertip bruises. Maybe I wanted to be normal, but I didn't know how.

"I'm sure you have."

I was ushered inside to the kitchen. As I sat down the adrenaline rushed from my system, and I went into a panic. "He protected me. He can't die."

"We'll do what we can, but from what I saw that was one nasty wound."

I ate on autopilot, drank the coffee Arianna forced down me, and time passed in slow motion. I tried to sneak in to see how he was doing, but Arianna barred me each time. I took a seat on the floor opposite the door to wait. Finally, it opened and a man who didn't look old enough to drink walked out removing gloves.

"We got the two bullets out, stopped the bleeding, but he

lost a lot of blood. With his size and physical condition, I'll give it fifty-fifty he'll recover."

It wasn't much, but it was something.

"Can I see him?" I asked.

"We're getting him cleaned up, but you can go in. We did what we could. He's your responsibility now." He left without another word, and I stood.

I walked slowly into the room to find two teenagers changing the sheets and then pulling a clean yet dingy blanket over Sorenson's bare lower body. I looked away in embarrassment until the teens left.

Grabbing a chair from the corner of the room, I dragged it to the side of the bed. All I could do was sit and wait.

I was still in shock that he put himself in danger for me. No one had ever done that before. I knew it was because I was his responsibility, but I sighed as I reached out and pushed dark, silver threaded hair back from Sorenson's weathered face.

The grim lines of his features were relaxed for the first time since I met him. His chest rose and fell evenly, I took that as a good sign or hopefully it was. I wasn't one to have faith in positive things. I hadn't had a lot of nice experiences in my life. I relaxed back in the uncomfortable chair and crossed my arms over my chest. I lifted my feet to the bed and settled in to wait.

As the hours passed, worry built as he made no movements on the bed. Arianna and the man called Doc assured me that my friend—I didn't correct them—was doing well. My eyes felt like sandpaper, and my head began to nod, my pointed chin touched my chest as exhaustion overtook me, and I couldn't fight the exhaustion and adrenaline crash anymore. I fell asleep hoping he'd be awake when I opened my eyes.

SEVEN

YURI

MY HEAD SWAM as I awakened in the dark. The events of what happened crashed into me. I tried to sit up, but it felt as if my body was weighed down and I couldn't move my arm at all. That didn't stop excruciating pain from radiating all the way to my fingers. I needed to find Josh.

"Easy, you don't want to tear your stitches."

A slightly raspy female voice came from the other side of the room. I forced my head to turn to find a petite woman standing beside the curtain-less window. The moonlight shimmered in her silver hair, and I tried to remember if I'd met her before. Did he call West to tell him what went down?

"Where?" My voice broke as I dropped my head back to the thin pillow.

"Josh called in trouble...needing help."

"Is he okay?" I asked as she pushed away from the window and came to offer me water. Most of it dribbled from the corners of my mouth as I realized how thirsty I was.

"Take it slowly. You lost a lot of blood." She took the cup from my lips. "If you look to your left, you'll see for yourself if he's okay."

I canted my eyes to the left and saw him curled uncomfortably in a chair. His thin arms wrapped around him. I'd noticed he did that when he wanted to comfort himself. The kid might think I didn't know anything about him beyond his file, but in the days that he was in my care, I'd studied him.

"So, tell me why I shouldn't kick his narrow ass for bringing a cop to me?"

Her tone put me on edge. "I'm no longer an agent. I left that life behind months ago."

"He knows the rules and lied to me. It was by omission, but still a lie. It doesn't matter current or former law enforcement."

"I was supposed to protect him during the trial. His ex's father is a Senator, and there's evidence he's dirty. Josh may know something and not even realize it."

"Politicians are always dirty, even the do-gooder ones. So, you're saying the Senator sent someone to rid the world of Josh for something he may know?"

I wasn't completely sure, but that wasn't an amateur hit team, and the younger Cross didn't seem like the one to have contacts with Mercs. Yet, that also didn't mean that both men weren't in on the attempt to take the kid out.

"My gut said it was a professional hit, but it could just be the kid's ex wanting to do away with a witness. Or just finish the job Cross started."

Calling him kid kept my distance. I couldn't give in to my baser urges. He wasn't up to taking me on.

"Josh isn't a kid, hasn't been one for a very long time. The name's Arianna."

"Sorenson, Yuri."

"Yuri, I'll keep your former law enforcement status to myself, and I suggest you do as well. We'll let Josh think he fooled me."

"You his mom?" I asked and listened to her snort. His file was pretty clear that he had no relatives. The information I was able to glean from his background checks, his mom lost custody after an attempt to drown him a few days after bringing him home. Then it was just a long line of foster homes afterward where the cycle of abuse continued until he'd run away to live on the streets. He'd probably thought it was his best option to survive.

"In a sense, his along with countless others. Yuri, I'm the one they all call when they're out in the cold."

"You run a safehouse." It wasn't a question.

"Among other things. It's taken me decades to earn the trust of the kids who need my help. Don't fuck that up. They need a safe place with no questions asked or judgment. You'll find your oversized wounded ass left on the side of the road to fend for yourself."

"Where's my vehicle, gun?" I asked.

"We left it at the pickup point and later sent someone to drop it off to be found in the city. By now, it's probably in an impound lot somewhere, or your fed friends are tearing it apart for evidence."

"You've done this before."

"I've lost count."

"Is the kid physically okay?"

"Except for the adrenaline crash and malnutrition, he's doing okay. I'm surprised he even held it together long enough to call me."

"I've got to contact the agent in charge of his protection."

"Once you're able to get around on your own we'll take you back to the city. While you're here, you won't have any contact with the outside. Calls can be traced. I have quite a few abused men and women hiding from their abusers. I won't put them in further danger so you can make a call. When you're able to leave, we'll give you a drop-phone, and you can call whomever until your ex-cop heart is content."

"Fair enough. Why don't I feel more pain?"

"We're well-stocked, and we'll leave it at that. I hope you're not piss tested on a regular basis. I just gave you another dose. It should kick in soon."

I growled at her amused voice, and it must have awakened the kid.

"You're awake."

The relief in Josh's tone surprised me. I flinched as soft fingers stroked my hair and Josh recoiled and quickly moved from the bedside. I felt guilty as he dropped his chin and shoved his hands into the front pockets of his sleep pants—pants stained with my blood.

"Josh, let's go get you a shower and some fresh clothes."

The kid didn't look up as he nodded, and I felt like an even bigger ass.

"Go on, and I'll bring you some clothes while you're in the shower."

"Okay," he replied and then ran for it.

Once the door closed, Arianna spun on me.

"Quit being a fucking asshole. That boy's had enough of it in his life. Yes, he dates men that like to fuck him until he can't walk or beat him until he's nothing but a bruise, but he doesn't know any different. To him, pain equals love. I tried to change it and show him differently. It never worked.

"That boy sat beside you all night to make sure you were okay. There's a shower through that door. I already have clothes in there to fit you. If you don't want Josh's help, then I suggest you nut up and do it yourself. No one else around here is going to offer assistance."

With that, she was gone. Arianna didn't slam the door, but she might as well have. I knew I was an asshole, and I normally didn't mind being called on it. Although Arianna's voice reminded me of my mother's, and it made me feel guilty. No matter how many times I said I was going to try to be nicer—that it wasn't the kid's fault—everything in me wanted to ravage him and keep him as far from me as possible.

I hugged my right arm to my stomach as I tightened my abs and pulled to a sitting position. My head spun and nausea churned in my gut. Lying still on the bed had led me into a false sense of security, and now I was paying for that. Breathing deep through my nose and out through my mouth, I sat still until it passed. The whole process took forever as I had to repeat the breathing until I stood and weaved my way toward the open bathroom door. A nightlight dimly shined inside, and a neatly folded pile of clothes lay on the back of the toilet.

A box of plastic wrap caught my attention, and I groaned thinking about removing the bandage and wrapping the wound so it was kept dry. I refused to ask for help though, especially from him. If it wasn't for the job, I would keep the kid as far away from me as possible.

I tried not to think about what Arianna said or what was in Josh's file. I didn't want to feel protective of him beyond him being an assignment. I couldn't deny my attraction. It was there from the first day I'd met him. I closed the lid of the toilet and sat down. Weakness wasn't an option for me, and the pull I had toward Josh was impossible.

"Sorenson?" My name was softly spoken and preceded an equally quiet knock. "Are you okay?"

"I thought you were taking a shower, kid." Exhaustion made my voice gruffer.

"Already done."

The door I'd partially closed slowly opened, and I looked up. Josh's unruly wavy hair fell damply around his heart-shaped face. He was too pretty. I cursed myself for noticing again. Delicate and meant to be taken care of, spoiled, and corrected in equal measure. I was just glad I was in too much pain for my body to respond to him because I hadn't taken time to drag the blanket off the bed to cover my nudity.

"Do you think you can make it on your own?"

"I don't know, but I've got to get cleaned up and change the bandage."

I dropped my chin to my bare chest. Blood was dried in my thick chest hair and that, with sweat, my skin was beginning to itch. I nearly jumped out of my skin when soft, delicate hands rested on my shoulders.

"Let's get the old bandage off, wrap it in plastic, and I'll stay in here while you get cleaned up."

"What do you think you're going to do if I fall?"

"Call for help," he stated.

"You do that quite well."

"I didn't know what else to do. Arianna was the only person I could think of I'd trust."

"This place and her weren't in your file." I looked up in time to catch Josh shrugging.

"It's off the grid, always has been. People come here for sanctuary or to get help to disappear."

"Why didn't you come here instead of staying with Cross?"

I observed him as he reached for scissors and started carefully cutting the gauze from my shoulder. Whatever they gave me still had my head fuzzy but definitely didn't take away from the discomfort. After meeting Arianna, I decided some things were best not asked about.

"I don't think it would've mattered."

"Why?" I asked. Maybe it was the drugs making my usual walls crumble, but I was curious.

"I asked for it..." he said then hesitated. "It's what I deserved. Everyone thinks so."

"Bullshit," I growled.

His downcast gaze made me lose my cool. My hands flexed where they rested on my bare thighs as the urge to soothe him became overwhelming. I hissed through my clenched teeth as the tape snagged in my chest hair and caught on the stitches where the blood had dried to the bandage.

"Sorry, I'm trying to be careful."

I heard the tears in his voice, and I lifted my uninjured arm to pinch his delicate chin. He gasped, and his eyes flew to mine.

"It's fine. Don't apologize. You did great in getting us somewhere safe. I'm proud of you." I dropped my arm back down as it began to shake.

His cheeks turned pale pink, and he finished removing the bandage, then cleaned around the wound with antiseptic. When he seemed satisfied, he wrapped my shoulder and bicep in the plastic wrap. I wrapped my hand around the back of his knee as he started to spin away to turn the knobs.

"Thank you."

"Y-you're welcome."

I released him and leaned back against the tank, trying to gather my strength before I attempted to shower. The tiny room was filling with steam.

"You'll feel better after you clean up. I always do."

I ignored his statement until I could correct him more thoroughly and struggled my way into the tub. I tried to put his presence out of my head as I made a half-assed attempt to clean myself. Cool air blew across my skin as the curtain parted then closed, my eyes opened to find a fully clothed beautiful boy staring up at me through a fall of wet hair.

"What are you doing, boy?"

"Well, this might go better with some help."

I didn't even feel the hot water hitting my wounded shoulder as slender soapy hands scrubbed over my chest and around to my lower back. Josh pushed his beautiful, slim body fully to mine. My cock was against his flat stomach. The damage done to my body didn't matter when I had to lift my arm, and he slipped behind me. He washed every inch of me except for a very insistent part and just when I thought he'd skip it, his forehead rested between my shoulder blades and slick hands stroked along my firm cock. I barely suppressed a groan as my foreskin pulled back from the sensitive head of my dick. My head fell back as his other hand washed my balls.

"Shit, boy, ya might not want to be playing with fire right now," I warned and growled when he broke all contact with me and then he was out of the shower, leaving me to finish rinsing off.

"I gotta go change."

His squeaky yell made me grin, and I knew I was in trouble.

"I guess the boy is gonna leave us hanging."

It took longer to get dried off, bandaged and clothed than it had to make it into the shower. I brushed my teeth with a toothbrush and travel toothpaste that was left next to my clothes. Cupping my hand, I drank water to fill my empty stomach and realized I needed food, protein, and some coffee. My boots were bloody, so I made my way from the room to find my boy or my reluctant hostess. Then I needed to plan what happened next and that had nothing to do with getting the broken boy into bed.

EIGHT

I STOOD on top of the porch's roof. It was flat and where everyone came to smoke cigarettes or whatever. Usually, it was deserted during the day. That's where I came to hide from my embarrassment.

"Is there a reason you've been hiding from your man?"

Arianna's voice took me by surprise but shouldn't have. I glanced over my shoulder in time to find her slipping out of the storage room window. Yuri wasn't the only one I'd avoided since the shower incident. In my gut, I knew she knew who he was. I didn't like lying to her. She'd always come anytime I called which hadn't been often in the last three years. At one time, I'd even had her come get me when I'd run from Vernon the first and last time.

"He's not mine."

My inappropriate thoughts about him had grown over the days that he'd protected me. I shouldn't even speculate what it would be like for him to touch me, if he'd love on me like all my forbidden fantasies of someone good who cared if I felt more than pain.

"Boy, anyone who saw how tore up you were—"

I waved it off and brought my attention back out to the overgrown forest, and the high fence beyond. "He got hurt protecting me."

"What's really bothering you right now?"

"I helped him in the shower, and I touched him." I knew any man who got his cock stroked would react. It was just the way bodies responded. But he'd been warm and firm, and I'd liked how hairy he was, the slight softness of his belly. He was so big that my head fit right under his bearded chin.

"You know it's okay to touch people we like and who like us back."

"He doesn't like me back. My heads all fucked-up. He's been...nice to me."

She stepped up beside me, but I didn't turn to look at her because this wasn't a conversation that I wanted to have face to face. I knew it was cowardly. I was a good fuck or punching bag. I wasn't known for my bravery.

"Nice and that's a bad thing?"

"Maybe in the shower I wanted to be more than nice to him." I felt stupid like I was trying to talk to my mom about sex or what I thought it would be like.

I'd lost my virginity at thirteen for a warm place to sleep. I hadn't liked it, and the man was old enough to my grandfather, with yellow teeth and foul body odor. That night, I'd rubbed my skin until it was raw with water so hot that I could remember the scalding and blisters. That began my unhealthy obsession with sex. Fucking made the violence less severe, or it was a night not spent in an overcrowded shelter or a hot meal when my belly was empty. My options had changed when I met Arianna, but I refused to run to her every time I had what equated to nothing more than a skinned knee.

"There's no shame in that."

"But what if I can't be normal?"

"Josh, look at me." The care in her voice made me glance at her. "I won't say you shouldn't feel whatever way you are, but sometimes we don't get normal. I never wanted to be a mother or wife, but in the end, I have a houseful of kids with a revolving door. I take care of them when they're ill or hurt. I make them disappear when they're ready.

"One day you're going to find a new normal. Someone that loves you so gently that the others from your past are no more than memories that'll fade with each kiss and cuddle, every smile just for you. One day, your normal might be a cranky, older, former federal agent who could use a little extra personal grooming."

I snorted and covered my mouth to hide my smile. "The night Vernon came home, I pretended everything was life as usual, but I had a bag packed. I'd hid it in the cleaning closet because he never went in there. I was going to run and find my way somewhere else."

"Who says you can't have that now? I can make you disappear."

"But what about the man after me. The next one who might not make it out."

"It's gonna sound selfish, but you can't worry about them. This is your life, and that is theirs."

"No, if he goes away, he can't hurt anyone else. My life won't be a waste."

"Then I'll support you however, but I do have one piece of advice for you."

"Yeah?"

"Go talk to Sorenson. He's not exactly happy right now. Apparently, you went AWOL."

"Shit."

She bumped me with her shoulder.

"You're going to be okay, and you know you can always call

when you're out in the cold. I'll have you on a plane or south of the border before anyone even knows you're missing."

"Thanks, Arianna. I'm sorry I brought him here, but...I didn't have anywhere else, and he couldn't die because of me."

"Just don't do it again. He's not bad. Maybe a bit too cranky for my tastes. A bit too...Dominant. But that might just be your type."

"I'm never looking him in the eyes again."

"Maybe he likes to bend his boys over instead—"

"I'm going inside." I rushed through the open window with her laughter following me. Dinner was over and the kitchen probably scoured, but there were always leftovers for late arrivals or people who worked nights to help with paying for their oasis.

Rumors were Arianna had plenty of money to fund this place for several lifetimes, but everyone liked to help out, chores, food, or finding meds to help with the clinic she ran. They always had a doctor or two that volunteered for exams and tests. Sometimes emergency rooms weren't an option. I entered the kitchen and went for one of the two fridges.

"Figured you had to show up for food sooner or later."

I spun to find Yuri in the shadows sipping at a beer, and I couldn't tell from his expression what he was thinking.

"Sorry, I needed some time to myself."

"Make yourself dinner, and once you do that, we need to have a long talk."

My hands shook as I did what he ordered and made a plate from whatever leftovers, then heated it in the microwave. I went to grab a beer because I felt I'd need it.

"You'll have milk or juice."

I started to argue until I saw his brow raise and I snatched a bottle of juice from the fridge, and then collected my plate. I sat at the table, and I watched him approach. He was favoring his shoulder.

"How's your shoulder?"

"Better. Over the counter pain pills are dulling it, but I think I'll survive. A couple more scars aren't going to bother me. Don't pick at your food...eat."

I took small, even bites, between tiny sips of juice. A sob caught in my throat as I realized I was waiting for him to tell me I was done like Vernon had. He'd only allowed me enough to keep me alive but starved enough to be too weak to fight—to protest my treatment.

"Use your words, boy."

"I was...I was waiting on you to tell me I'd eaten enough."

"I'm not him, and you're about twenty pounds underweight for your height. You need food to gain it back. Doc is going to give you a physical tomorrow."

"I already went to the doctor. They said I was healthy, and all my tests were negative."

"But I wasn't there, and you need to make sure you're gaining enough weight and getting the proper nutrition."

"Yes, sir."

"Good. Now, for what we have to decide on. We have to move out. I need to make contact with West and find out who the hell sent a Merc hit team to our room. It's not impossible that someone followed us, but I was always careful. Also, I wouldn't put it past West to sell me out. It wouldn't be the first time he let sensitive information slip. We're going to get lost for a bit. As soon as I find out where my vehicle with all my stuff in it is."

"It's only been a few days. It might still be parked where they left it."

"Let's hope."

"Was that all you wanted to talk about?"

"For now. We're going to have another talk when we're somewhere we won't be interrupted."

"Oh."

"You don't know me, Josh, but I'm a man who doesn't take kindly to a boy hiding from me. Let's make sure that doesn't happen again."

"Yes, sir."

"Now finish your dinner and then we have to talk to Arianna about a ride out of here."

All I could do was nod, and I felt his gaze on me, watching every bite I took, and I occasionally glanced at him to find his complete focus on me. His big hand was wrapped around the beer bottle, and he was picking at the label with his thumbnail. I sensed as if he wanted to say something, but he was holding back. I didn't see him as a man who stayed silent if he had concerns on his mind, but I was too scared and nervous to ask.

We hadn't started off on the right foot. We finally seemed to have a truce going. But there was still another talk coming, and that's what scared me the most. Would he punish me for touching him like that? He was warm and solid—gruff, but I was sure he'd never put his hands on me in anger. Although, I'd thought the same at first with Vernon. He'd done everything right those first few months until he had me trapped and then I had nowhere to go.

I didn't want to believe Yuri was the same, but I didn't have much faith in the goodness of men because I knew their depraved natures more thoroughly. If he did want to hurt me, all I could hope was he'd make my death quick and not draw it out.

NINE

YURI

THE TIGHT T-SHIRT pulled at my bandage, and I was ready to be out of borrowed clothes. I was hoping I wouldn't have to visit every impound lot tomorrow when we made our way back to the city. There wasn't anything I couldn't replace, but right now there wasn't time for that. I leaned on the corner of the house and focused on Josh. Seeing him there had changed my perspective of him. The shy smile when someone teased him. A weight had lifted off of him since we'd arrived, and I debated whether to leave him there or not.

He'd be safer, but my brain protested that I needed him close. If he was out of my sight, I wouldn't be able to contact him since no one was allowed cellphones, and calls were timed to make sure they weren't traced. Arianna was strict about the secrecy of the safehouse's location. She'd only given me a number and a list to show which locations for pickup. Not having constant contact with him wasn't a choice for me.

While I trusted they could keep him safe, my possessiveness suddenly latched onto an inappropriate boy for the Daddy Dom in me, and I couldn't justify anyone else watching him.

I grinned as a man not bigger than Josh, picked him up from

behind and spun him around. His laugh and smile were so free and happy. But I knew the minute he spotted me all that shine would dull, and he'd be back to collapsing into himself.

Too many enemies waited for us. Unknown dangers that we could pass on the street without knowing they were waiting to stab us in the back. I'd rather be between him and them when it happened. I had no doubt that it would. Too many powerful players were on the field, and I needed to narrow them down. That meant leaving the bubble here and hitting the streets to draw them out.

"I arranged a ride for you." Arianna came out of nowhere.

I'd learned that she preferred to keep people on their toes—not allow them to get too comfortable.

"You love sneaking up on people."

"Reactions are raw and without artifice. One of my people said your SUV is still safely parked in the same place, but he moved it to a second location. You have quite a few tickets to pay."

I glanced at her to find the corners of her eyes crinkled with amusement. "Of course I do."

"You sure you don't want to leave him with me?"

"I should, but"—the sigh that slipped from between my lips sounded weary—"I can't."

"I understand, but one phone call and we'll pick him up."

"Appreciate it."

"Nothing I haven't done for him before. Just make sure that he doesn't turn into a piece of ass."

I snorted. "Like I told him, I'm not his ex. But when the time comes, we'll talk about that privately."

"Fair enough. I have a friend. Runs a flophouse. Building is barely up to health code, but he's got rooms down for *repairs*. Which is code for a safehouse. He said one of them is mine if I need it for one of my *kids*. Just tell him Arianna made the reservation. The owner knows too many secrets for the cops to come nosing around. The police chief likes to bring his side chick around a few times a week."

"You might come in handy."

"You're not my type."

"The feeling is mutual."

Even in the midst of a dangerous situation, I felt more myself than I had since I retired or quit, whatever people wanted to call it. Growing up, I'd lived in low-rent housing, Mom barely making ends meet with her assistance, and Dad turned out to be useless. This wasn't the place I grew up, but cities like these were identical. Same dealers and crime bosses, uptown or downtown, people were all the same. Nothing separated people more than how many zeroes were in their bank accounts. Entitlement oozed from the pores of the rich, leaving a foul stench in the air.

Perception colored how we viewed ourselves and others. Dirty or shabby clothes made us slump into ourselves as if the world was there to push us under their heels. And if you were seen as upper-middle-class or upper-class than there was no glass ceiling keeping you down. No limit to your dreams. I was stuck somewhere in between expectation and reality with nowhere to go but sideways.

"You'll be good for him."

"What?" I asked. I'd been so lost in my thoughts that I'd forgotten she was there.

"For Josh. He accepted whatever he could get. Never thought he deserved more."

"We have some behavioral correction to work on, but we'll get to it...after I make sure he's safe."

"Man, you're not keeping it in your pants until he's safe. Alone in a motel room with condoms and lube, you'll be lucky to leave to find the people after him."

"I'm so overwhelmed by your faith in my abilities."

"I trust you to keep him safe, and that's high praise coming from me. Doc wants to check your shoulder over one more time before you leave to make sure it's still looking good. He may have mentioned you're one tough bastard. Anyone else would be dead."

"I'll take him up on the check, and he's gotta look at Josh, too. I want to make sure he's still on track to getting healthy."

"He's put on a bit of weight since I saw him last. He's starting to look like the teenager I used to know. I have to get some work done. We have a supply run coming up."

I nodded and then brought my attention back to him. I had to agree he was beautiful in that delicate way that elegant men had. Men I'd secretly wanted, but I was always too rough around the edges to keep them. Last time I'd given into my urges, it was an unsatisfying fuck of two dominants fighting for control. Yes, I got off, but it wasn't what I'd call a repeat-worthy performance. I craved trust and submission, someone who knew I was in charge and put the decisions in my hands. Being in my forties, I may as well be elderly. I didn't mind being someone's Daddy, but I wanted that one boy I'd been waiting on for too long.

To be honest, I didn't know if that was Josh. Only time would tell, and the shift in our dynamic would help us both open up to sharing—to mutual respect. We'd have to work on his skittishness, and only a gentle hand would work, maybe some praise. I remembered his blush when I'd told him I was proud of him. My gut said it was the first time he'd ever heard that from someone, especially a man.

First step, I would have to repair his confidence and self-worth. Gently instruct him on recognizing the good things about himself. Despite what she thought, while sex was definitely on my mind, it wasn't the most important thing. Intimacy was key.

Getting him used to touch that wouldn't end in pain. I wouldn't say he wouldn't earn punishments, but that was only after I figured out the right rules for us.

That would happen soon enough. We needed to make plans to move out in the morning, and before we could do that, my boy needed a checkup.

"Josh," I called out, and I hated when he froze with his smile slowly slipping from his lips. "Doc wants to see us."

I patiently waited as he said goodbye to his friends, and then I strode to the front porch. I motioned for him to precede me, and while he still wasn't confident with someone at his back, he obeyed. Ascending the front steps, I caught up with his slower pace and placed my hand on the small of his back.

"Do I have to?"

"Yes, this will be the last time I can get you checked over. He wants to examine my shoulder, too."

"Okay, but I hate doctors."

Which meant he probably didn't have a regular one and that wouldn't do. If he was going to be mine, I'd need to take care of that. I suppressed a smile as my brain tried to formulate a plan of finding him doctors and a job, but I'd need office help so I already mentally marked something off the list.

I led him through the house to the downstairs den turned makeshift clinic and knocked on the open door.

"You two finally showed up. Figured I'd have to lock you down in the morning before you left."

The kid looked too young to be a doctor, but from what Doc said, he'd finished with his residency and had taken a job in a free clinic a year before.

I was so fucking old.

"Who's first?"

"Check Josh first. My shoulder can wait."

My boy tried to protest, and I shut it down with a single

look. His bratty eye roll made me want to grab his chin and warn him what that behavior would get him with me, but I reminded myself tomorrow would be soon enough.

I leaned back on the wall beside the door and watched as Doc ordered my boy to remove his shirt. His ribs and breastbone were no longer prominent. The scars from his wounds were still raised, reddened marks on otherwise creamy skin. I observed everything from the weighing to the checking of vitals. My possessiveness was becoming worse as another man touched my boy—they were closer in age and similar in builds.

"Sorenson, it's your turn. Remove your shirt."

I'd gotten the damn thing on fine that morning, but I wasn't so sure about taking it off.

"I'll help." Josh's words muffled as he put his shirt back on and walked over to me.

I seated myself on a nearby chair to make it easier for him. It was the bastard in me, but the way his hands shook reminded me of our shared shower and his touch. His timidity turned me on.

He eased the fabric over my head and off my injured arm. I grimaced at the sudden pain but ignored it in favor of keeping him calm.

"Now, let's see the damage."

I kept my gaze on Josh as Doc examined me, no matter how much I said I'd wait, I had to admit that our hostess might be right—he'd be too much temptation to resist.

TEN

JOSH

I WAS EXHAUSTED, and the sun hadn't set yet. It was nonstop since Yuri had yelled for me to get out of bed, waking up the other people on the cots around me in the communal room. Everyone had booed and hissed as they threw pillows and anything else in his direction. And I was still reliving his laugh in my head. It was the first time I'd heard any sound other than growls and the occasional grunt that he used when he was unhappy.

The day was filled with renting a storage unit for his SUV under a fake identification. He'd packed a duffle with everything he'd need, including his weapon, and shoved my own borrowed backpack inside. Arianna had packed it for me with some clothes and personal care items. She said there was a surprise for me too. I was kind of scared. Her smile was more of a smirk than I'd ever seen it.

He said we'd utilize taxis and public transport until he could arrange for another vehicle. I was standing in the lobby of a motel that hadn't seen a renovation since the forties. I was familiar with places like this. They only rented by the hour and were perfect for our needs because no one asked questions as long as the cash didn't run out. He was talking to the night clerk, and I turned away as the other man glanced at me.

Yuri told me to put my hood up, so I was sure my face was too shadowed for the clerk to see details. We'd been checking the news regularly, and other than a short segment on a suspicious shooting at the hotel, neither of our faces were shown.

I jerked as Yuri bent down to grab the bag and slung it over his uninjured shoulder.

"I have the key, come on. We're on the fourth floor."

He put himself between me and the desk as we made our way across the lobby to the stairs. The old elevator had an *Out of Order* sign taped beside the open doors. I didn't get as winded as we took the stairs. I felt stronger and lighter, but still had the edge of fear that never went away.

That part of me which had always been ready to die was rearing its ugly head. I was too much trouble. The effort he was putting in to keeping me alive was a waste of his time. I swear I tried to banish the thoughts with maybe dreams of something happier, but it just wasn't working.

He told me to stop when we reached the door of our room, and I waited while he opened it. He pushed the door open, and when I entered, I was shocked. The room was pristine, yet still had the same crimson printed walls with red carpet. Yet, it looked and smelled clean.

"At least we won't need a round of antibiotics when we leave."

I hid my smile as the door clicked shut, and he passed me to place our bag on a luggage rack. I wrung my hands as he slowly took off his hoodie, and I chased the play of shifting muscle beneath his tight t-shirt. My fascination with him needed to end before I got hurt. I knew he wasn't like Vernon or the others. Yet he knew my past and what I'd allowed to happen to me. How could a man treat me differently when he knew how the others had used me?

My body craved something I hadn't had in my life—yearned for a possession that had nothing to do with pain. But I also wanted to be owned and taken care of; have the harder decisions made for me. That just showed me I had to hide that I was losing a piece of myself to him. As gruff and hard as he appeared, he took care of me, and I felt that was skewing my perception—seeing more than I should.

"Relax and settle in. I'm going to run out to get us dinner and a few things. Anything special you want?"

"No, I'm fine. I'll probably just pass out after I eat."

I stepped back as he removed his sidearm and flipped it around so the hilt was toward me.

"I'm taking the key with me. If the door starts to open and I don't announce it's me, you shoot, do you understand me, baby boy?"

"I've never—" Anything I was going to say froze on the tip of my tongue as he spun to stand behind me. His broad chest flush to my back. His breath was teasing my ear.

"You hold it like this."

His big hands wrapped around mine.

"This is the safety...don't take it off until you're ready to fire. And don't aim or wrap your finger around the trigger unless you're willing to shoot."

My chest tightened, and my stomach twisted with a swarm of butterflies as he made me hold the gun by myself. It wasn't the heaviness of the weapon that made me nervous, no, it was the spread of his hand across my belly. I knew I was imagining things, but it almost seemed as if he pulled me into him a bit more.

"You need to understand that depending on the circumstance, you're going to have to protect yourself—even if that means leaving me."

I was too afraid of his reaction to protest, but it didn't help that he was warm and solid. His presence was so comforting that I could easily become addicted if I wasn't already. Vernon or whoever was after me were second to him, and that was dangerous. If I wanted to live, I needed to remember that he was only there to protect me. He saw me as a duty and nothing more.

Pain was my addiction of choice. In my fucked-up wiring, agony meant love. Bruises and cuts, a sore ass—all that meant I'd get the sweetly whispered *I'm sorry or I love you* and the lies that it would never happen again. A security blanket because it was normal and familiar, and that familiarity was a perverse safe place, in way.

Rough fingertips touched my cheek and nudged until I turned my head.

"Where did you go just now?" he asked, with his lips close enough to brush against mine.

I didn't even toy with the idea of lying to him. "That maybe it would be better to give in."

"Baby boy, we've come too far. You're exhausted and stressed, but I'll make sure everything is taken care of. Now, I want you to get in your pajamas and keep the gun with you, and I'll be back soon."

For a second, I almost thought he was going to kiss me, but then he lifted his head and pressed his mouth to my forehead. He held still for just a moment before he was moving away and all I heard next was the door closing. With shaking hands, I laid the gun on the bed and sat down beside it. I rubbed my chest to alleviate the tightness.

I was doing what I'd always done, latching on and when it was time to move on—when he grew tired of caring for me—he'd leave. I was only a job. His sense of duty kept him close—urged him to protect me. *Run*, the single word repeated in my head, driving me insane and ordering me to do what came natural —hide.

He was good. He felt clean. A fantasy of those protective Prince Charming characters in the fairy tales and romances I'd secretly read. He was a trap. All I could remember were all the others were nice too. They'd done everything right. Gifts and dates—outwardly, they sold the neatly wrapped package of the happily ever after that wasn't meant for people like me. We were broken and unlovable, only worth the effort for the reward they received—the power to abuse our bodies and minds. And we...I so willingly accepted the scraps for the other times.

The sweet times. Those teasing kisses and loving touches, which ended the split second we were naked. In the end, the gentleness faded until it was no more than a specter, the humili- ation and pain taking its place. I told myself I deserved more. I soothed myself with the blackness as I was tied or held down, fucked for their pleasure—their release. Only I was left cold, bruised, and aching. For me, pain was love, and I knew no different.

Did men see me and see the shattered thing that existed beneath the too-thin body and pale skin? Did I wear some sign that told men that I was so starved that they could do what they wanted with me without repercussion? I wrapped my arms around myself, started the gentle rocking as I sought the only comfort I'd had since birth. I fought the sting of tears, but no matter how much I pushed them back while berating myself, they still made hot tracks down my cheeks. Falling drops that soaked into denim and cotton, drying proof of how inhuman I was. I would always be nothing more than an object for other men's use and never the beloved I wanted to be.

ELEVEN

YURI

I FLIPPED the hood of my hoodie up and shoved my hands in the pockets as I made it down the crowded sidewalk. Twisting my upper body to avoid the passerby connecting with my slowly healing shoulder. Doc was concerned it was becoming infected and gave me some antibiotics to hopefully stop it before it started getting bad. I had worse concerns than that—keeping my boy alive long enough to take the Cross family down. Even if that meant stepping further outside the law than I already had, then so be it.

I needed to find out what part West played in the attack. He could be innocent for all I knew, but we'd gone around too many times for me to trust him. I'd needed the money, so I'd taken the case.

We'd be locked down most of the time, so I needed to pack in supplies so I didn't have to hit the street often. Plans swam in my head, and those unknown variables I'd ignored came back to haunt me. I weighed the old adage the enemy of my enemy was my friend, but I needed to find out who exactly that was. Who had a hard-on for the Crosses?

I popped into a convenience store for drinks, bread, peanut

butter, some packaged snacks, and even some candy to keep my boy happy. With my head down, I checked every aisle. Occasionally, I would look up to see if the cashier paid too much attention. He was too busy on his phone, and the cameras had no cords. Store owners liked to think the possibility of security footage would derail a perp's plan to rob a place. I threw things in the small basket. While Arianna covered the room with a favor, my funds weren't limitless, and I could hope that the Feds hadn't frozen my accounts if I needed them. Hitting an ATM was a risk depending on response time, but if I needed to then, I'd head to the other side of the city.

I got enough to last a day. Sneaking out at night for something more substantial was safer than hitting the streets during the day and chancing that local law enforcement had a *Be-On-The-Look-Out* issued for us. I could blend, but my boy was way too pretty for that. I grabbed a cooler because I checked for ice and drink machines before I'd left the motel. With that in mind, I asked for quarters back when I got my change.

I hung the cooler from my good shoulder and carried the plastic bag on the same side. When I exited the store, I looked for a place to grab a quick, hot dinner. I scoped out a few dive bars in the hopes of a payphone. The era of cellphones sent those the way of the dinosaurs, but I knew a few places still had them. If I kept the call short enough, we'd be harder to trace. Cellphone signals could be triangulated, and that would lead the authorities too close for comfort.

I walked into an Asian restaurant and ordered several safe options. I knew Josh wasn't picky about food, but I also didn't want to make him suffer through an upset stomach.

While I waited, I thought about the contacts I needed to make. Calls would happen tomorrow, though. Tonight was about supplies and sleep. He'd looked exhausted by the time we'd made it to the motel. The stress was wearing us both down.

I knew it was hitting him harder, though. I'd been doing shit like this longer than he'd been alive, and I knew what to expect.

But there was one thing I was having a hard time handling—how badly I'd wanted to kiss him before I'd forced myself to leave the room. His eyes, with their long pale lashes, had dropped to my mouth for a second, and his breath had hitched. Being noble wasn't exactly in my personality. I also couldn't let my hormones take over. Once he was safe, maybe I'd see if he was a Daddy's boy, but until then, it would be too much like taking advantage.

He was starved for gentleness and tender control, but his needs were colored with gratitude. My mind warred with my body over that. I hadn't crossed the line with an assignment, and I didn't plan too, but I wasn't seeing him as a witness in need of protection.

My number was called, and once again, I took the bag on my good side. The slight weight of everything was causing the stitches in my opposite shoulder to pull. I knew I needed to take it easier. I snorted as I realized that wouldn't be anytime soon.

My legs felt heavier as I made the return trip back to our room. I needed food and sleep as much as my boy did. Part of me was worried that I was too old to bounce back like I used to; that I wasn't going to be enough to keep him safe. I didn't want to think that his trust was misplaced, but while I didn't have many insecurities, getting older was definitely one of them.

I took the stairs, and when I reached the room, I knocked and announced it was me. When I unlocked and entered, Josh held my weapon in his shaking hands.

"It's okay, baby boy. You can put it down."

I felt guilty as he seemed to lose all strength and barely put the gun down without dropping it. I approached the bed.

"Here, go through everything, and I'm going to grab some ice. Don't wait for me to eat, okay?"

He nodded, and I left the room for the ice. And again, wondered if I'd done the right thing.

I WOKE with a start automatically reaching for my gun on the bed beside me. I stayed silent as I listened for what awakened me. Feminine giggling preceded a slamming door farther down the hall. When I relaxed, I noticed the weight against my side. Neon and flashing lights came through the thin curtains, and my boy was curled up with his back to me. He was hugging my good arm to his chest, and his head was resting on my bicep.

I turned and pulled his slim body fully against mine. I groaned as he wiggled his ass against my groin, trying to get closer. His thick hair was still slightly damp from his shower. That meant I hadn't been asleep long. I tightened my arm around him, and his little sleepy moan was nearly my undoing. And what happened next broke me.

He tried to move from my embrace, I allowed him to roll over, and he searched for my mouth in his sleep. The soft curves gave under my firmer, thinner lips, and I relented but only for a moment. I fisted my hand in the fabric over his ribs. His sexy little whimper urged me to do more, but I didn't. The kiss had no finesse or heat, just comfort. I softly brushed his lips with mine, whispering between each for him to go back to sleep. And he tucked his head under my chin and nuzzled my bare chest with his cheek.

Grabbing the comforter and sheets, I pulled on them to cover him to his pointed chin. I grimaced and bit back a groan, knowing I needed more pain medicine. But I didn't want to wake him up by slipping out of bed. His slender fingers fisted in my thick chest hair, and he let out a sigh as the tension in his body eased away.

I wondered what he was dreaming about. I'd listened to his nightmares enough at the hotel. The panicked screams. The loud sobs and pleas that easily traveled through a closed door. I knew he'd talked to Arianna, but when this was over, I needed to make sure he found someone to talk to and work out his past. To take the pressure off my shoulder, I turned onto my back and smiled as he followed. He sprawled across my chest, and while it wasn't ideal for me in the event that I had to protect him, it seemed to bring him comfort, so I let him do as he wanted. Maybe he needed comfort more than protection, and I decided at least for tonight we were safe.

So I cuddled and suffered as he straddled my hips, pulling the covers all the way over his head. I'd realized that's how he liked to sleep. I'd yelled for him that morning because I hadn't seen him in the sea of cots covered with blanket wrapped cocoons. I rubbed his back and felt relief that his spine wasn't as knobby.

I relaxed and tried to make myself go back to sleep, but he was too close—too vulnerable. And I reminded myself that I was going to protect him from the people after him, but also me. I wouldn't push until it was right for him. That didn't mean I wasn't going to start getting him used to what having a Daddy Dom was like. I had plans, but when they came to him, I wouldn't push until he learned that love and sex weren't all about the pain inflicted on him.

TWELVE

JOSH

I AWAKENED from the best dream I'd ever had. One of the few times I hadn't come to with a scream and then I froze as I found myself draped over Yuri. My thighs were on either side of his hips, and I tried to slip to the side without being noticed only to squeak as a very strong, large hand squeezed my ass to keep me in place. This was so not good. I bit my lip and tried again only to be stopped by a deep growl that rumbled the chest under me.

All I remembered last night was falling asleep as far on the other side of the bed as I could get. I'd never really shared a bed with someone before. Usually, when the man I was with went to sleep, I left or found a couch or a portion of the floor to curl up on. At Vernon's, I had my own tiny room which he locked me in every night.

This was the first time I'd ever cuddled with a man, and I wasn't sure it was a welcomed act. I needed to get away before he woke up. His opinion was important to me, and I didn't want him to think that I'd done this on purpose. I planted my hands beside his ribs and then lifted onto my toes.

I was able to get an inch between our bodies before my hips

were slammed back down onto a very impressive bulge. My brain went to forbidden territory as I remembered exactly what he felt like in my hands. He was uncircumcised, and I was fascinated by it. Wondered what the loose skin would feel like on my tongue. I shut down my thoughts before something bad happened.

"Shit," I whispered and started the attempt again.

"Baby boy, what do you think you're doing?"

His gruff question had me lifting my gaze to his and realized he was very much awake. "How long have you been awake?"

"Maybe an hour or so."

"Sorry, I didn't realize—" My apology ended when I noticed the corner of his mouth pulled into a smirk. It made the laugh lines at the corners of his eyes deeper.

"Asleep, you didn't seem to mind rubbing on me."

I surged to a seated position and stared down at him. "I was sleeping. I could've done anything." His smile got wider. "What else did I do?"

"Nothing, but we have shit to do today so get on up."

He smacked my ass and rolled out from under me, dumping me onto the bed. I hurriedly crawled off and followed him. I was too shocked by the grin and the suddenly playful attitude to protest the swat.

"What did I do?" I demanded.

"You get pretty affectionate. Now, are you going to watch me piss and demand to know every grope you didn't get to enjoy?"

I narrowed my eyes, and I slammed the door as he let out a loud snort. I liked him better when he was a grumpy bastard, and I stomped across the room to grab the last soda in the cooler. I opened it, and I found the ice mostly melted and nearly cried at a seeing a small can that said double espresso. When we were at the hotel, he'd made sure I had a few cans in the fridge every morning. I knew he was only working with a limited amount of cash because he didn't want to keep going back to the storage unit to raid his stash, so he didn't have to make the special effort to buy me one. I popped the top and chugged it. I moaned in pleasure.

"I think I remember a sound like that."

I pivoted on my toes to find him leaned in the doorway of the bathroom with the shower running.

"Eat some food. I'm getting in the shower, and then we have to run out to make some calls."

He stepped back into the room and didn't close the door all the way. It wasn't as if I hadn't seen him naked. I'd joined him in the shower. Yet, I tried not to think about that too much, but those thoughts were going to get me in trouble. He'd think I was trying to get him to fuck me. I didn't want that. One I day, I wanted to be loved on by someone who cared.

Instead of trying to sneak a peek through the crack in the door, I made myself a peanut butter sandwich and grabbed a bottle of water. I took a seat on the end of the bed and turned on the TV to check the news.

Days had passed, and still, there wasn't anything to tell us if we were wanted or not. The judge had postponed the trial until they could find me. Vernon had made bail. He lived in a penthouse in one of the most expensive properties and ran his father's former company since the man had been elected to the Senate. Vernon had all the comforts his wealth could afford.

I heard the door open, and I glanced over my shoulder with a torn-off piece of sandwich inches from my mouth. Water beaded in his chest hair.

"Your stitches look better."

"Still hurts like a son of a bitch, but I've had worse. Anything new?" he asked as he passed me to dig out clothes from the bag.

The bastard had the nerve to drop the towel and expected

me to think. Next time I got the gun I was going to shoot him myself. I snorted at my thought.

"Care to share the thought?"

When he bent over, his muscled cheeks flexed as he stepped into his boxer briefs. He straightened and then turned before he covered his thick cock.

"I thought about shooting you myself."

"That isn't an odd occurrence. I usually get that reaction." He spoke as he adjusted himself.

My hands flexed at the sensory memory of the silky skin along his shaft and the heaviness of his sac. I forced my attention back to the TV, but if he asked me what I was watching, there wasn't any chance I'd be able to tell him what I was looking at. I'd never remembered being this fixated on someone. It was new and scary, and I was unable to process that. I didn't know if I could.

By the time he took the seat next to me on the bed, he had on his jeans, and he dropped his boots onto the carpet between his feet.

"So anything new?"

"No, um, still nothing about us and no more mention of the trial since the other day."

"I'm not liking the media blackout. A trial this high-profile should be all over the news, local and national. Especially with a Senator's son involved."

"What does that mean?"

"It means that more than likely, every cop and fed in the city has pictures of us."

"What are we going to do?"

"Unfortunately, I'm going to need to contact West. I thought maybe it was time to find an ally in the media. Juicy story and some reporter will cum in his pants to get it."

"You mean Vernon Cross' fuck boy who can't bend over fast enough for every man who hands him a fifty."

"Josh!"

I flinched at the harshness in his tone. He didn't even sound like that before he liked me. I dropped my chin and wrapped my arms around myself—my lingering fear flaring back to life. Shame filled me as I waited for the hit I expected. The humiliation wasn't for the fear, but for the fleeting relief of something familiar—normal.

And as became his habit, he pinched my chin and forced my gaze to his.

"Most people think I'm a bastard, unfeeling or whatever, but there has been no time since I've known you that I would put my hands on you in anger. But if I have to correct you, I will. This is your one warning. Don't speak about yourself that way again."

He never looked away from me. There wasn't any anger just, I guess, disappointment.

"We all make mistakes. Sometimes we don't know any different, or we need to survive, but we learn and adapt. Do you understand?"

I could only nod, and it seemed to satisfy him. He brushed his mouth across my forehead. His longer beard tickled my nose, and I realized he was looking a bit more like a mountain man than when I first met him.

"I think you need a trim."

"I do. Maybe you can do it for me later."

"Me? No, I'll mess it up."

"It's a beard. It grows back. You can trim it later. I have my clippers in my bag."

"Okay," I agreed but hoped he'd forget about it and do it himself. "What are we doing again?"

"You're going to get all pretty and then we're going to the

library to send and check some emails, do some research. We have to pick up a prepaid phone for emergencies only. Then we hit the dive bar down the block to use the payphone in the back to make a quick call. Now finish your sandwich. I'll get you something better for lunch and dinner. Maybe we'll hit the store to find something to keep you occupied."

He leaned forward to put on his socks and boots. I almost offered to help but didn't know if he'd appreciate it. He'd taken care of himself before I came along. I found I liked doing things for him—taking care of him. When this was over, we'd go our separate ways, and I'd have to learn to handle life without him. Maybe I'd go work for Arianna. She was always looking for people to help around the hideouts in the city, transporting the runs who were on their way to disappear. I had some server experience, but nothing else.

I didn't want the same life. I wanted different, but did I have it in me to be someone better? A thought flashed in my head that I wanted to be different for him. Yet, I had to do that for myself. I needed to find the person I was meant to be and not the one borne of necessity.

THIRTEEN

YURI

MY BOY WAS LEANING his rounded ass on my back as I tried to focus on doing the searches I needed. I shook my head because he'd been attached to me in one way or another since we left the motel a few hours earlier. He'd even hooked his fingers in one of my belt loops as we'd walked down the street. I tried not to read too much into it, but I was selfishly pleased I was his comfort item.

I'd barely slept at all last night with him rubbing his slim body all over the top of mine. He also had this obsession with nuzzling my beard. He'd appeared so cute that morning demanding to know what he'd done. Teasing him could become an addiction.

Suddenly I had a delicate chin resting on my shoulder. "What are you searching for?"

"Reporters that make too many waves." I didn't look at him as I continued scrolling. We needed a reporter that was as paranoid as we were. Which I didn't think would be too hard to find. More than anything right now, we needed allies.

"You're not searching the case?"

"No, only because they might be tracking keyword searches.

You do know the term Big Brother is Watching?"

"Yeah, grandpa."

I lifted my arm to fist my hand in his soft curls. "Don't get bratty, you won't like how it turns out."

"Y-yes, sir."

His stutter again gave me an odd satisfaction. I really shouldn't find his discomfort around me adorable. I needed to rein myself in. I promised myself not to do anything about my attraction until my boy was safe. That wasn't exactly working for me.

"Can you type with more than two fingers?"

Just what I needed in my life—a huffy, bratty boy. I was about to ask if he could do better but then he was seating himself on my thigh. He handed me his milkshake.

"So, what are we searching for?" he asked.

"Reporters that covered the most scandals in the city. Comfortable?"

"Apparently, I did more in my...sleep."

He darted a glance over his shoulder and batted his pale lashes, and then he went to typing. His slender fingers flying over the keys and I let him work. Maybe he needed something to keep him busy.

"Walter Moffett. Veteran journalist with thirty years of experience being a pain in the butt. There's the second candidate, Ernest Burton, seems a bit shady."

"Shady isn't a bad thing." I had to admit that the shadier a person was, the safer it was to trust. In my experience, people who appeared too good to be true normally were.

"No, but Moffett would probably give more professionalism to the case. He's covered every scandal in the last three decades. Seems he doesn't care who his target is."

I scanned several articles that he clicked through. Moffett was a kindred bastard spirit. "Wait, what's that one? Don't open it." I pointed at the screen and saw an article that outlined the case against Cross, but the one below it caught my attention. The senior Cross had allegedly gotten caught with his dick stuck in a barely legal babysitter. "Do you know anything about this?"

"No. Vernon kept me away from his family. Dirty little secret and all that, but I do know that he wasn't shy about having affairs. According to a conversation I overheard, the old man was usually a lot more careful, and they were bitching about someone going for a payday. Vernon laughed a bit and said that was a check the whore wouldn't be around to cash. I'm going to end up just like her, aren't I?"

His pale, watery gaze turned to me, and I raised my hand to gently pinch his chin. I'd found it was the best way to get his attention without making him cower. My boy was coming out of his shell a bit—if his emerging bratty attitude was any indication. I didn't want to hinder the development of his true personality.

"You're going to be fine. I promised, didn't I?"

"You're using your Daddy voice on me. That's not fair."

"Daddy voice?"

"The one that says everything is going to be okay. That the monsters aren't real, but we both know that isn't true."

I wrapped my arm around his waist and leaned forward to continuing scrolling through articles. I wasn't in the habit of lying, especially not to myself. Strange thing was, I wanted him to be safe—feel that all was right in the world for a few minutes even if it wasn't the case.

"You're right, but I can't guarantee we won't be running for months."

"I'd prefer it not to be that long."

"Then we're going to have to get to work. This isn't exactly how I wanted to start retirement."

Minutes passed as more research only gave us more questions that needed answers. I used a piece of scrap paper from beside the computer and wrote down the number for us to call from a safer location. We might need to come back here at some point.

I started to worry the longer he didn't speak.

"Yuri?"

"Yes, baby boy?"

"I really like your Daddy voice."

I shook my head as he grabbed his empty cup and wiggled to get off my lap. I let him go when he gave the cutest growl. When I chuckled, he nudged me with his hip and disappeared. As fucked-up as it sounded, my retirement might be turning out more fun than I planned. Well, except for the hitmen, the holes in my shoulder, and questionable no-tell motels. But other than that, it wasn't too bad.

SMOKE BURNED MY NOSE, and my boy coughed beside me as we walked into a strip club several blocks from our current hideout. I'd gone to my storage unit and retrieved one of my suits, but I had taken my boy to get pretty. I'd dug into my emergency cash supply I kept hidden in a safe. Everyone needed an escape plan. Also, he'd been pouty most of the afternoon, and I wanted to spoil him.

I placed my hand on the small of his back and nudged him forward and led him to a booth all the way in the back.

"Get in," I ordered, and he slid in. I followed and tucked him under my arm.

"How long do we have to wait?"

I'd contacted Moffett earlier and told him we had some information on the case, but I hadn't mentioned my boy's name.

When I'd told the reporter that I was in law enforcement and on the case, he'd asked where to meet us. The tricky part was the meet. It always was. You had to trust the lure of the information was enough to have them keep the other parties honest.

"He said ten, but we showed up early to check the layout."

I kept my voice calm, and I didn't tell him that I'd recon'd several locations for the meet. This particular club had a broken alarm on the back exit where I'd seen dancers sneak out back for smoke breaks.

"If something goes wrong, I want you to run for the back exit. Take a left in the alley and circle around the block and back to the motel. If I'm not there by morning, take my bag, go to the unit to grab all the cash and call Arianna. Do you understand me?"

The argument in his eyes was clear, but I wouldn't let him disobey. I'd already arranged for her to get him out of the country. My trust in her was tentative at best, but I knew he trusted her completely. I didn't want him to have to run the rest of his life. Yet that didn't mean he wasn't going to need to prepare for that.

A server in a short skirt and a dress shirt knotted just beneath her breasts approached with a tray, and I got us drinks. A top-shelf bourbon for me and a soda for him. Mine was all for show. I waved off the offer of a dance, private or otherwise.

"Why did you turn it down?"

"Not interested. I can call her back if you'd like one."

"No."

I scrubbed my hand over my mouth to hide my grin at his widened eyes. I forced my focus out onto the room. Smoke shifted through rays from neon signs. Music seemed to pulse under my feet and in the booth frame. It was like any other club I'd been in over the years. In my undercover days, I'd worked the door in a place just like this one.

"What are you thinking?"

I started to answer him but paused as the drinks arrived, and the server set them on the small round table. I threw a large bill on her tray. In my distraction, I started drawing circles on his hip and liked when he rested his slight weight against my side.

"I was thinking about the last time I worked security. I'd been undercover for six months. I was hating life. But one of the dancers needed protection as they prepared to take her into protective custody."

"Do you miss your job?"

"Occasionally. You do a job that you were good at for a few decades it takes some...adjustment."

He tucked his face against my neck, and I turned my head to nuzzle his smooth cheek.

"Maybe I should just run, Yuri, maybe you'll be safe then. He just wants me. I can turn myself in. It's not like I haven't been waiting for it to happen."

"Boy, you will do no such thing. I'm telling you now, you'll start thinking about the consequences of your actions when it comes to disobeying me."

He jerked back, and just as he was about to say something, a strange male voice came from my right. I turned to find a tall, slender man about a decade older in a wrinkled dress shirt, loosened tie, and a messenger bag slung over one shoulder.

"Sorenson, and if I'm not mistaken, Josh Clarkson himself. This is more interesting than you made it sound on the phone."

He took a seat on the other side of Josh.

"So what do I owe for the exclusive?"

"An exchange of information. Someone wants us dead, and you want a story that'll keep you on the front page."

"I can find those stories everywhere."

"Not one with the possibility to take you into syndication.

Can't be ready to spend the rest of your life covering the same old bullshit year after year."

"Rumor has it, the defense is trying to get the case thrown on account of due process. They can't postpone the trial forever when the star witness pulled a disappearing act. Can't help but wonder if one of those rumors is true."

"And what might that be?"

"Seems he's"—Moffett nodded toward Josh—"ran off with his bodyguard. Replacing Cross with an older model. Sounds like downgrading to me, but boys sometimes have minds of their own. What have you got for me?"

"The entire story, exclusive including anything on all the Cross family that Josh knows and for that, all you have to do is keep us informed on what they're not saying on the news. Also anonymity for Josh. No mention of his name. Don't want to make him a target a second time when the story runs."

"Exclusive, all the dirty laundry on Senator Cross and his son. Is that a deal you're willing to make, kid?"

I studied his expression, saw him warring with his need for self-preservation and for it all to end. No way in hell this was easy on him. Everything could end, and the thought of him dying sent a cold chill down my spine. It wasn't the first time I'd thought we wouldn't make it out. I had the new scars to prove it.

"Yes, I just want my life back."

"And what life is that? Back to being Cross's toy or—"

I saw the look he sent my way and felt the way my boy tensed. For Josh, I don't think things had changed completely. My boy still had that mindset that he deserved what he got from Cross.

"The or." Josh's voice was so quiet, if my focus hadn't been on him, I wouldn't have seen his mouth form those two little words.

"Then I guess we have a deal."

FOURTEEN

JOSH

THE OR. What the hell had I been thinking? I cursed myself as I unbuttoned my baby blue dress shirt that conformed to my slender upper body. As I stripped it off, I studied myself in the bathroom mirror and draped the fine linen over the edge of the sink counter. I traced the fading scars that covered my chest and stomach. A few were still sensitive as I stroked the raised edges of tissue. The ones on my face had been superficial but still left pale pink lines on my cheeks and forehead.

"They're healing nicely."

I jerked my eyes to the right in the mirror to find him watching me—an odd expression in his eyes. I wondered what he thought of me. His attitude toward me had shifted, but I still feared he saw me as he had the night I was led into his office. In his opinion, was I still the pain-addict whore that everyone made me out to be? At the club earlier, I'd almost felt—normal. Like a well-adjusted man curled up against my date.

I mentally shook off my thoughts, and my brain started to focus on other things. Yuri's unbuttoned shirt exposed the thick hair on his chest and stomach, and his tie was hanging loose. To keep from getting caught, I returned to my perusal. My stomach was no longer concave, and my ribs didn't show through my pale skin. My face was filling out, and I didn't look like a skeleton. I knew I had more weight to gain in order to get up to fighting weight as he called it.

"Yeah."

"What's wrong, baby boy?" His grumbly voice was low and soft, yet seemed to fill the room effortlessly.

"Just remembering."

"Remembering what?" he asked, as he entered the bathroom and stood behind me. There were several inches between us, but I could still feel his body heat—his overwhelming presence—and my weakness called to me to lean back into his strength.

Something inside me was sick and rotten. I relied on him to keep me safe. He did little things that weren't necessary. Like the espresso, candy, or letting me pick a show on TV. They were stupid things, but men didn't do nice things for me just out of the kindness of their hearts. It always came with a price.

"Talk it out."

Resistance was futile when his hands rested on my hips and he flexed his arms, pulling me back to his larger frame. The slightly coarse chest hair tickled my skin, and my gaze flew to his. Nothing in his expression gave away his thoughts. He was as stoic as I remembered. That emotionless mask made me warier. While I didn't think he'd physically hurt me, emotionally and mentally he could destroy me.

"Do you think I'm the same as I was when West dropped me off?"

"Boy," he growled in my ear. "Did you ask for these?" he asked, as rough fingertips tenderly stroked the scars I had only minutes earlier.

"No."

"Or this?" He cupped my chin, and his thumb moved along the scarred curve of my lower lip.

"N-no." I gasped as he did it again before dropping his hand back to my waist.

"Did you ask to be used so brutally?"

"I don't think I did, but it's what I expected."

"Expectation is a funny thing, baby boy. It can shift and become something different. We're a malleable species. We evolve...change. What we were yesterday isn't always who we are today."

"Do you believe that?"

"I don't normally say what I don't mean. If you've noticed, I'm a bit of an asshole."

I saw my lips quirk up at the corners in the mirror and caught him smiling as well. I felt lighter with him and was terrified that my gratitude molded my emotions into more than they were. Whatever that was, it was headier than agony, infinitely more addictive, and I feared it showed in my eyes.

"You're a bit grumpy." Even as I joked to cover my discomfort, my body involuntarily gave into the yearning to lean back slightly into his strength—his warmth.

"Diplomatic of you. What do you want for dinner?"

"I'm not picky about food, but I'd love a burger and fries."

"As you wish. I'm going to change into street clothes and run out for a few. Behave while I'm gone." I froze as he gave me a quick hug and then disappeared returning a moment later without a word to place his gun on the sink. "I want you to lock the door, okay?"

I answered with a sharp nod as I glanced from him to the weapon. He seemed satisfied that I'd listen, and he backed out of the small room.

"Take your shower," he ordered from the other room, and I stepped back enough to peek as he changed into a t-shirt and jeans. He lifted and turned his head. "I thought I said behave, little man."

"I was going to close the door." I closed the door a little too forcefully, locking it and then finished stripping.

I waited until I heard the room door slam before I turned on the shower and stepped inside. I didn't linger in the shower, quickly washing my hair and body. Yuri made me think about sex, and that was dangerous. Every man I'd known in my life would've taken advantage of being straddled and rubbed on, but not him. He was messing with my head, that's all it was. When everything was over, I'd move on and find something different, maybe a new city where no one knew who I was.

I rolled my eyes as I turned off the water and stepped out into the steam-filled bathroom. I dried off and wrapped the thin fabric around my hips. When I stepped out into the main room, the door opened, and he was back.

"Perfect timing. I called West. I'm meeting him tomorrow."

"What about me?"

"You'll stay here, where it's safe and be ready to run when I don't show back up."

"You have to stop telling me to run. I'm safer with you."

"No, you would've been safer staying with Arianna."

That hurt and I hid my expression. "Then why didn't you leave me there?" I yelled as I strode to the bag to dig out pajamas.

He grabbed my arm and spun me around, and the pissed-off expression was one I'd seen before. Without thought, I jerked my arms up to protect myself. He grabbed my jaw in his large hand and squeezed, forcing me to look at him.

"I'm telling you right now, I won't ever touch you with the intent of hurting you, but I'll bend you over my knee. Look at me, Josh." He barked out the order. "It's my job to take care of you. To make sure you're safe. Now, while it would've been safer for you to stay with her, I promised you I'd take care of you. You won't question me again. You're going to stay here so that you can run to Arianna. I've already arranged for her to get you out of the country if needed."

"I don't want to run."

His grip loosened and he slipped his hand to the back of my neck, then he tugged me close. I felt his lips brush my wet hair, and he hugged me to his chest. I twisted my hands in the thick, fabric of his hoodie. I rested my forehead on him and took a deep breath. The longer he was silent, the more nervous I became.

"Neither do I, but I need to talk to West, and I don't want you caught in the crossfire if something goes down. I don't trust West, but on the off-chance he's an ally, I need to know what he does."

"You going to leave me the gun?" I pulled back far enough to give him the bratty fluttering lashes that seemed to make him roll his eyes but still laugh.

"Yes, I'm not going to leave you completely unprotected. Now, are you ready to get in your pajamas and have dinner?"

"I'm starving." I broke contact with him and bent to pick up my clothes from where they fell. I straightened then made my way back to the bathroom.

"You're just going to use me as a body pillow later, why shy?"

I lifted my hand to flip him off.

"Baby boy, you don't want to do that."

I quickly dropped it back to my side and went into the bathroom, changed into my t-shirt and pajama bottoms, realizing too late I was wearing his clothes instead. I couldn't return for my mine since I'd made my dramatic exit. I hung up the towel and stepped back into the room.

"Now, my clothes?" His voice was amused as he laid out the food from the greasy bag.

"I'm already wearing them...you're not getting them back. I

require food with fat content and the possibility of clogged arteries."

"Good thing because the diner on the corner was the only place open."

He handed over my food and another milkshake. I bounced back to the bed and sat on the end, pulled my legs onto the bed and crossing them, sticking my milkshake between my thighs. He took the seat beside me and handed me the remote.

"Only an hour of TV time and then bed."

"Yes, sir." I found something to watch and slowly ate, paying more attention to him than whatever movie was on.

Maybe it was sick of me, but I was going to miss us being trapped together. We hadn't spent more than an hour away from each other in weeks. It was meals together, seeking him out for comfort and I was looking forward to another night of waking up curled against him. I tried to warn myself not to become attached. I feared it was already too late. That wasn't the worst part. I was falling for the grumpy, older man and wondering if I was going to let years of history repeat itself. My appetite fled, but I forced myself to continue eating to keep him from becoming suspicious. I was fucked and not in a good way.

FIFTEEN

YURI

I PULLED my hood up to cover my face and searched the area from my seat on a bench. From this position, I could see West pull into the parking lot and make sure he arrived alone. I'd made sure Josh was awake, fed, and ready to run if needed. He'd looked so sweet when I'd gently nudged him until his eyes opened. In that lazy space between sleep and wakefulness, his expression appeared so free. He'd smiled up at me, and I'd fought my need to kiss him until the sweetness became something else. I'd slipped from the bed as quickly as I could without making my retreat feel like a rejection.

There weren't any options for me but to keep him alive until I could claim him for mine. It was inappropriate—lines being crossed in the adrenaline of staying ahead of our enemies. I was too old for him. Too much of a bastard. Yet, I couldn't deny my brain agreed with my body. I craved him. And I didn't understand why. I'd protected hundreds of people and never lost my professionalism. I couldn't afford to lose my calm.

I had to admit mistakes were always possible. Some things couldn't be accounted for, especially in these situations. Not all the players were identified. I could guarantee that the Cross family was at the top, but both had more money than brains. They could pay anyone to take care of their problems. I just didn't know who else we were fighting. What enemies we couldn't see that were hidden behind a smiling facade.

Game time.

West stepped out of a plain sedan. He was dressed in the cheapest suit I'd ever seen him wear with a few days' growth of beard. Even from a distance, I could tell he didn't look like he'd slept in weeks. I didn't get up to approach him. I scanned the lot for vans or vehicles that stood out, but nothing really hit me. I was big with going with my gut. It had saved me from plenty of fucked-up operations in the past twenty years.

I shifted and felt the comforting weight of my forty-five holstered at the small of my back. Stretching my arms along the backrest of the bench, I watched him sit down. He jerked as if his nerves were on edge—every man built on my scale wearing a hat or a hoodie earned extra scrutiny. I chuckled as I noticed him cursing beneath his breath.

Easing from my seat, I headed in the opposite direction that he was focused on. I flopped down beside him.

"Hello, West."

"Goddammit, Sorenson. What the fuck is going on?"

"Why don't you tell me? I don't like people trying to shoot my fuzzy ass off."

"I got nothing. All I know is all hell is breaking loose. The defense is cocky as fuck, and the prosecution is fighting like hell for the postponement. All I could tell them was our main witness was in the hotel, there was a significant amount of blood in the stairwell leading to the garage. It disappeared where it looked like y'all got in a vehicle, and it could mean that Clarkson or you were dead somewhere."

"Took two to the shoulder trying to get Josh out. We're laying low for now, but we can't hide forever."

"Then fucking come in...both of you. We can set you both up in protective—"

I laughed coldly at his suggestion that I put me and my boy out in the open. If they found us in protective custody the first time, they sure as hell would the second time around.

"Who knew Josh was in my custody?"

I'd rather keep my focus on him to read his face and body language, but I kept searching the area for signs of danger. Being out in the open like this had its advantages. No one could approach, and midday meant witnesses. Yet it was also dangerous too. I just had to hope that West was truthful and hadn't sold me out.

"Me, the prosecution, no one else, I swear, man, I didn't burn you."

"What did the room service guy say?"

"He went MIA before the cops arrived. His boss said he never came back from delivering food to your room that night. He could be on some beach by now."

"That was a professional team. Not some group of street thugs. They had military training. They were aiming to fucking kill, and if I hadn't moved as quickly as I had, you'd have found my corpse somewhere. How much time do I have?"

"Two weeks. Yesterday there was a meeting in the judge's chambers, they have fourteen days to produce the witness, or he's ruling it a mistrial. And we both know what that means."

"It's over, and Josh won't survive. I need information, West, and I don't want any of your bullshit."

"Whatever you need, it's yours."

I shot him a suspicious glare, and he held up his hands.

"Man, we're cool. Whatever you need. I feel my days are numbered. You know my record isn't pristine...they're just waiting for an excuse. Clarkson was my responsibility, and taking down the Cross family would be a coup to the higher-ups."

I reached into the pocket of my hoodie to slip the list of names and information I needed. I required addresses and case files. Pretty much I needed everything on the case. I handed it over, and West opened it.

"You'll have to give me a few days."

"I'll contact you again then to set up a drop."

"Do you need anything? More cash?"

"I'm still on the clock, remember?"

"Shit."

I roughly laughed as I pushed to my feet and left without another word. I pushed my hands into my pockets and kept my head down as I took the long way around to the bus stop to take me to the first transfer. I had an hour to get back to my boy before he was supposed to leave. The cellphone was with him so that he could make the calls he needed to get Arianna to pick him up.

If needed, I'd hunt him down, but I knew he'd wait until the last second before he left me. The heaviness of exhaustion began to weigh me down. I'd stayed awake to watch him sleep for longer than I should have. Knowing that things could go tits up in a heartbeat, I loved that my boy found comfort in my presence. He reached for me in his sleep if I even moved an inch away.

I turned right out of the northern exit of the park and circled around to the bus shelter. The next one would arrive within minutes. I blended into the crowd as I waited, and as soon as the doors opened, I entered and passed over exact change for the fare. I found a seat in the back and settled in for the fifteen-minute ride and then I'd walk the rest of the way. Which hopefully would have me arriving right on time. I'd told him two hours.

He was beautiful, and I wanted to make sure that he made it out the other side safe and happy. Even if that was somewhere unknown to me. I'd never had permanence or known what it was like to sleep with an adorable boy in my arms. Maybe I was getting spoiled with the newness of that. He was a gift that any Dominant would crave. Naturally submissive, but he fought his nature because the men in his past had abused the blessing that he was.

Yes, I was hired to protect him—to keep him safe, but before this was over, I wanted the boy to know his worth and what he should demand of the Dom he chose. The touch and praise, then gentleness and spoiling was a plan. Behavioral correction that would leave him stronger and more willing to demand what he needed from the man who claimed him.

And while the thought of another Dominant touching my baby boy infuriated me, I knew it was a lesson I could tenderly give him. Every good Dom read their sub's needs. He was in the infancy of his transformation, but the potential I saw in him already took my breath away.

I almost missed my stop and jogged off the bus before the doors closed. He made it so easy to get lost in my thoughts, and that wasn't something I could afford when I was away from him. He depended on me. I'd earned his trust. I wouldn't betray that for anything. The walk cleared my head and allowed me to check for anyone keeping too close of an eye—maybe following. I went one block farther and then circled back around. Checking the time, I knew I was ahead of schedule, so I ducked into a corner store to grab my boy a couple cans of the espresso he liked.

Quickly I was making my way up to the room. I knocked on the door to signal it was me, and I entered. My boy's expression was bright and happy, completely open and trusting for me.

"Hey, baby boy."

"How did it go?"

"We'll have the information in a few days and some more cash. I have enough to keep us going, but I told West I was still on the clock."

He giggled as I passed and he took the paper bag I held out to him. I caught his happy dance as he peeked inside, and then I was stripping my hoodie over my head. Without thinking. I placed my weapon on the nightstand, moved to the end of the bed crawling onto it and wrapped my arm around my boy's waist pulling him with me. I tucked him to my side and kissed the top of his head, as I only half-watched what was on the television.

"I'm going to miss this," he said as he nuzzled me.

"What's that?"

"Sleeping with you. I feel safe, and I shouldn't."

"Josh, I want you to feel safe. If you don't, then that means I'm not doing my job right."

He drew circles on my chest, and that simple, innocent touch did more for me than any man in my past.

"Is that all I am...a job?"

I pinched his chin and drew his gaze to mine. "You are more than a job, even when I was trying to be a professional hard ass, you got under my skin, baby boy. But that's a conversation for another time. I need a nap. You're very distracting when you sleep."

At his shy smile, I resisted the lure of his lips and instead brushed my mouth to his forehead. He turned away from me to hug my arm to his chest and rest his head on my bicep. I bit back a groan at his rubbing and let out a gruff, relieved sigh as he settled in. As I started to drift off, I fisted my hand in the cotton over his ribs to make sure he couldn't sneak away. Our time was running out, and if things didn't work out as I hoped, I wanted a few memories to keep.

SIXTEEN

JOSH

I COVERED my smile by shoveling another spoonful of yogurt in as he snapped the paper and growled from his seat in the cheaply upholstered red velvet chair. Sneakily, I pulled the remote from under my thigh and kicked the volume up another two notches on my cartoons. The rumbling from the other side of the room grew louder and the paper crinkled in his fists.

That morning he'd said that we needed to hide out, it was going to take a few days for Moffett and West to get us the information for the next phase. I was bored. An odd brattiness began to transform my skittish nature into something different. It was a freedom I never experienced in my life, and while I'd fought it, I was coming to savor the idea of safety—more as a concept than a reality. Maybe delusion was a better word for it.

Shooting another glance at him, I started to reach for the remote again, and the newspaper hit the floor.

"You touch that button again, little man, we're going to have some issues."

"What issues?"

"You're going to end up with a sore, red ass."

"You wouldn't."

I realized I shouldn't have said anything because he was out of the chair and stalking toward the bed. To evade him, I rolled off the opposite side and set my yogurt cup on the nightstand.

"Yuri, um, I'm sorry."

"You had your chance for regret about three previous volume increases ago. I believe three times is more than enough for you to think about your decisions. Now it's time for correction."

"I didn't do anything."

I jumped back a few steps as he made his way around the bed, but stopped at the foot of it. He calmly sat on the edge.

"Push your pants and underwear over your hips to mid-thigh, then lay across my lap."

I backed away and used my hands to cover my ass. His expression left me no way to argue with him—the hardness of his features. Fear tightened my chest, but he didn't appear enraged, just irritated with me. As if I'd broken some unknown rule. Would the pain make me regress? Would I become the thing I was before I'd met Yuri?

"Use your words, baby boy."

"What if I go back?"

I knew I didn't have to explain what I meant. It was there in his eyes when he watched me. He understood me better than anyone else, not even Arianna who knew all my secrets. It was another experience with him, though. He'd only known me a matter of weeks, knew nothing more than what was in my file, but he knew me.

"Correction is different from abuse. Correction isn't always about physical punishment. Sometimes it's sitting in a corner to think about your actions. Rules are to keep you safe and happy. I don't want to destroy your brattiness, Josh. It's a part of you that was suppressed due to the violence in your past. With that said, I believe I gave you an order that you need to obey."

I nibbled nervously on my bottom lip. I lowered my pajama bottoms and underwear but kept my crotch covered. I didn't want him to see.

"I know what you're hiding, and there's no shame here."

"Can I please stay covered?"

"Yes, you can."

His voice was so calm and soothing, and I wanted to hate him for that. I was envious of his coolness—of his strength. I approached him slowly and stretched out over his thighs, the comforter soft on my thighs and calves, my knees sinking into the mattress. He didn't touch or force me to comply. I fisted my hands in the quilted fabric. I jerked as the roughened pads of his fingers and palm spread out over my lower back.

A confusing combination of anticipation and terror kicked my heart into a painful overdrive.

"Josh, once this is over, we're going to have a talk. I was trying to wait until we were safe, but unfortunately, I'm a selfish man."

I parted my lips to ask for an explanation, but the sting of his hand connecting with my right ass cheek stopped me. I bit down on the inside of my cheek to keep from making a noise. A yelp slipped out when he repeated the smack on the opposite one.

"Actions have consequences. Rules are given for you to follow so that I know you're safe when you're not with me."

"You don't give me rules."

"And that ends...now. You will repeat each rule that I issue. Do you understand me?"

"Yes...yes, sir."

"Rule one...you will accept every compliment I give without argument."

His thighs flexed under my stomach, and his fingertips dug into my lower back before he struck again on each cheek.

"Repeat our rules."

A sob choked me, and I swallowed hard trying to clear the knot from my throat. "I will accept every compliment."

"You hesitate again, your punishment will take longer."

"Yes, sir."

"Rule two...you will always be completely honest with me."

The spanking intensified. It became harder to think. Tears stung my eyes, and I choked out the next rule. This sounded wrong, like permanence. A sweet promise I didn't want to accept. Yet, I craved that. I wanted that fairy tale that was colored with happiness and not the tales in their original and horrific versions.

"Rule three...you will never put yourself down."

I repeated as he told me to, but the compulsion to argue grew until I had to speak around the constriction of my throat. My flight response kicked in, and I tried to get away from the pain blooming in my abused cheeks. What had simply stung morphed into a fiery agony.

"Shh, baby boy, just relax. We're almost done. Just trust me a few more minutes."

I wanted to fight against the soothing nature of his voice. But I wanted to tell him I trusted him. Past and present fought for dominance, the acceptance of pain for love or correction as care. Caring was much more intense. Love was an empty platitude, words spoken in superficial apologies—the fleeting fuck as someone used you to get off. With the spanking came a scary lightness, relief, but I also felt outside myself.

"Rule four...you will no matter what, always take care of yourself first. Your well-being above everyone else's, including me."

The skin on my bottom felt hot and tight, and he struck the lower curves where they met my thighs.

"Get up and sit on my lap."

I slipped off his lap and went to cover myself, but his softly whispered no stopped me. I fisted my hand in the fabric and kept it in place so I wouldn't expose the scars that covered my pelvis, hips, and groin. He knew they existed. They'd been shown off in all their brutally explicit nature in photos in front of a packed courtroom.

I sat down on his thigh but quickly found myself cradled on his lap. His arm was a brace across the middle of my back. My head rested on his chest. The hair tickling my cheek and nose. I waited for it and wasn't disappointed when he pinched my chin to make sure I looked at him. The emotion in his eyes was intense, and I was trapped by that.

"Your safety means everything to me, and I need you to understand and accept that."

I hugged his forearm to my chest, and my eyes kept falling to his firm lips. My eyes fluttered closed as his calloused thumb stroked along my lower lip. Felt the pad catch on the scarred skin. A sigh slipped out when he brushed the gentlest kisses to my mouth, the corners, the bowed top one, and I sightlessly followed the warmth and care. No man had ever kissed me like that as if this was enough. That fucking me wasn't the end goal.

"Open your eyes. I need to see them as I finish with your rules."

And the rules were a seduction, none of them had anything to do with sex or getting off. The spanking didn't even feel sexual. It was just as he'd said, correction.

"Rule five...you'll tell me what you want or need at all times."

I repeated the rule and felt lighter—freer. There wasn't a suffocating weight on my chest forcing the air from my lungs. I stroked my fingers through the hair covering his pectorals. I felt more than heard his rumbling.

"Rule six...I can add rules as I see fit depending on behavior and circumstance without notice."

"Yes, sir."

"Now let me see who belongs to me."

He helped me off his lap, and I stood before him, his hands were clenched on his thighs. Barely an inch of fabric existed between exposure and modesty. Did I have the courage to take that step? This would be an acceptance of his ownership of me.

"What was rule number two, baby boy?"

"I would always be honest."

"That's right, so use your words."

"I don't want you to fuck me."

"And I have no plans to do so. My pants stay on, but yours need to come off...now."

I shoved them down before I could give it a second thought. I stepped out of them where the fabric pooled around my ankles. My fists were clenched as I fought my need to hide my body—the ugliness of it. I jerked my gaze upward as I heard the bed creak and saw him scooting backward until his back was rested against the headboard attached to the wall.

"Tell me why you're uncomfortable."

"My body is ugly. I'm too thin. I'm covered in scars."

"No, Josh, you're not too thin. Yes, you need to gain a few more pounds to get to a healthy weight, but you were kept starved as a way of control. You're slim and beautiful. Your scars are proof you're a survivor. There is nothing ugly about it. Our bodies change. No one can escape life or time. We're not meant to stay the same."

My body didn't respond to being nude in a room with a man I had started to stupidly fall for. The jaded part of myself forced myself to remember that when this was over, I would just be a fleeting memory, but what he'd shown me would last much longer. I was already too attached to my grumpy Daddy.

"Come here and lie down." He patted the spot beside him.

I hesitated but crawled onto the bed. My stiff movements giving away my insecurity. I laid down on my back and laced my fingers on my chest. My breath caught in my throat as he laid down and his strong hand curled around my bony hip.

"I'm going to spend a lot of time telling you just how perfect you are. Look at me, baby boy."

I opened my eyes and found his face inches from mine. The tip of his nose nudged mine, a smile flirting with the corners of his mouth.

"Now, open for me, baby boy, let Daddy in."

I gasped as his mouth came down on mine, and at that moment, nothing else existed.

SEVENTEEN

YURI

I WOKE up with my fingers fisted in the back of my boy's soft hair. We'd fallen asleep talking, and as the night progressed, he'd cuddled closer to me. When we'd gone through his rules last night, I knew he'd been shocked that the rules weren't about sex. Fucking was easy enough, in our modern age of internet and apps, a hook-up was a swipe away. My boy needed something else. He needed intimacy and care, and when I knew we were both free, we'd take that next step. Until then, I had plans for him.

Lifting my head from the thin pillow, I kissed the top of his head. We were going to have to work on this sleeping situation though. But I had to admit I wasn't averse to being his comfort item every night. Especially when I woke up with him draped completely over my body. It was playing hell with my libido, but I was a man who could control myself. He needed to understand he was more than a body to be fucked and abused. That when the time came, his pleasure was the most important thing to me. I wouldn't say I wouldn't show him who owned him, but I wasn't a sadist like the other men in his past.

I eased him off me and rolled off the bed. The sun wasn't up yet, but I needed to get going for the day. West should have all the files for me, and I needed to make contact with Moffett. I was ready to get out of this room, and I knew my boy needed some fresh air. He'd been stuck there for two days.

I crossed the room to our bag and chose our clothes for the day. I laid his out on the foot of the bed and took mine into the bathroom to grab a quick shower. After relieving myself, I stood in front of the mirror and used the trimmers to clean up my beard. It had started to turn shaggy. I was just using a razor to clean up my neck as my sleepy boy padded into the bathroom with his eyes barely open.

I finished up as he used the toilet and washed his hands. He wasn't a morning person, especially not without at least a few double espressos in his system. I chuckled as he moved behind me, his arms twined around my waist, and he rested his forehead to the center of my back. My amusement turned to a deep groan as he pushed his smooth skin to mine. He was still warm from bed.

"It's too early."

He whined, and I slipped my left arm behind me and patted his hip.

"I didn't make you get up, little man."

"You got out of bed. I want my body pillow back."

"Unfortunately, we have things to do today."

I felt his pout against my back, and then he was nuzzling me. He drew circles through the hair on my stomach.

"I get to go with you?"

"I think you need some time outside. We need to go to the library to check to see what Moffett has for us. Then we'll meet with West. He's getting me all the files." I wet a rag and cleaned the hair and shaving cream from my face.

I took his left hand and urged him to come around in front of me. Then I easily lifted him onto the counter. He wore only a pair of superhero briefs. His thighs parted as I closed the short distance between us. I lifted my hands to cup his jaw, and my thumbs beneath his chin tipped his head back.

"Will this be over soon?"

"I hope so, and then you can decide what you want to do with your life."

"What's that?"

"Not for me to decide."

"But...but...what if I want you to decide?"

"My sweet, bratty boy, when this is over, if you still want me to make decisions for you, then I'll do so." I lowered my head to kiss the pout of his bottom lip. "But first, we have to work on you finding yourself."

"Am I a project, some good deed to repair some Karmic debt?" His voice rose barely above a whisper. The question was colored with self-doubt and insecurity about whatever was going on between us.

Hell, I wasn't even sure what was going on.

"Do you know why I was so hard on you when West brought you to me?" He shook his head. "My father was a mean mother-fucker. He used his fists in place of words...emotion. Mom was completely subservient to him. She had nothing that was her own...not even thoughts. Her life was nothing more than a generational cycle of abuse. Everything about her screamed broken."

"I reminded you of her?"

"In some ways, yes, but it was more than that. The old man only came around enough to use her body and leave when she was no more than an inhuman mass of self-loathing. She accepted the abuse as her destiny. Love to her was the kiss of a fist. Love letters written in blood and bruises. She didn't survive to learn there was more than him. You are going to learn, change, and adapt. Before I make you mine, you're going to discover who you are. What you're worthy of demanding."

"Why are you so nice to me? You saw my file...what he did to me."

"The question isn't why I'm nice to you, say what you really mean."

"You're an ass—"

"None of that, you're deflecting. In your mind, you don't think you're worthy of someone, especially a man being nice to you. Wanting to touch you for reasons other than pain and humiliation. The things I could do to you, baby boy."

A rumble vibrated my throat as I stroked my fingertips down the smooth, flat plane of his chest and stomach. Goosebumps prickled his flesh, and I went lower until I tucked my fingers in the front of his briefs. I felt the puckered edges of scar tissue hidden in the sparse, dark blond curls at the base of his cock. He took the edge of the counter in a white-knuckled grip.

He was waiting for permission to move—to demand. And I wanted to tenderly break him until he begged me for what I knew he needed. We'd danced around this for weeks. Neither of us finding release. I brought my eyes back to his face, took in the slashes of red along his cheekbones and the way his pretty lips parted to allow for his quickened breaths.

I removed his underwear, a gasp escaped as his bare ass met the cool countertop. His dick fit perfectly in my hand. I fisted my free hand in his hair and jerked his head back. I barely pressed my lips to his as I jacked him.

"Da—" He brutally bit into his bottom lip to keep it in.

"Say it, baby boy, we both know who I am." My cock ached, fought against the confines of my boxer briefs, but he wouldn't get fucked by Daddy until I deemed him ready.

"Daddy," he whined as his body betrayed his caution, and he fucked my fist. The tip of his cock wet where it met my belly.

"Fuck, boy, I could get off just watching you. Look at me."

He opened his eyes and his gaze locked with mine. His thighs shook where they gripped my hips. Every want and need was right there in his eyes—every dream he was too terrified to voice. Without warning, his arms twined around my neck and wetness covered my lower stomach and hand as his hips stuttered as he found his release. A scream muffled against the side of my neck.

I let go of his dick and hugged him to me as he rutted in circles on my abdomen. I pulled back enough until my mouth could find his and we shared lazy kisses. My cock and balls ached, my body wanted the orgasm I denied myself. He was warm and relaxed in my arms. His lips curving into a tiny smile, and that was enough for me. This had been for him—pleasure given without pain or expectation.

"Did Daddy make you feel good?"

He hummed an affirmative and held onto me with all the strength he possessed in his slim body. A body I really wanted to take back to bed and love on like the world outside didn't exist. We didn't have time for that. We'd have plenty later when we were both free and he'd made his choice when it wasn't colored by gratitude or isolation. When this job was over, I'd set him free and let him come to me.

"Ready for the day, baby boy?"

"Nap time."

"No time for a nap, you can lay back down until I'm done getting ready and then it's your turn."

I lifted him from the sink and carried him back to bed. I laid him down and gruffly laughed as he tried to hold on when I attempted to straighten.

"Behave, and you might get some more playtime when we're done for the day."

As he was sprawling on the bed, he arched his beautiful

body and tried to tempt me to join him. As much as I wanted to, I forced myself away, returning to the bathroom to strip out of my underwear. I didn't wait for the water to warm and stepped under the cold spray.

I needed to break the cycle of his past abuse, but I was close to shattering myself. He was there for the taking and claiming. I could make him mine with a single word. I couldn't, though. I wanted his mind clear of fear and regret, to make the healthiest decision for himself. Playing with him even a little was drawing close to crossing a line. I never said I wasn't selfish—his first real pleasure was mine. No other man would ever have that, and it would always belong to me whether he was my little when this ended or not.

EIGHTEEN

JOSH

I COULDN'T HELP that my mind kept wandering back to what happened in the bathroom that morning. The touches he gave me took on new significance. I'd waited for him to demand I return the favor, but he'd just carried me to bed and went to shower. It was getting harder to remember that when this was over, he was going to let me go. That his care and lessons were only to teach me to demand what I deserved.

Unfortunately, what my brain and body told me I deserved was him. We were seated in a back corner that put the entrance in sight and an exit a few feet away. Like we'd done the last time, I seated myself on his thigh and typed in what he requested. Adding a few searches of my own. The one email he'd received was Moffett naming a time and a new place to meet later that night. Another address situated in an alley off a main strip where there was nothing but bars and clubs, a few cheap motels, and a couple abandoned warehouses. Still far enough away from our hideout that Yuri didn't seem worried.

We'd have to find a payphone to find out where West wanted to meet. We had less than two weeks before the case was declared a mistrial and it would be knocked back until new evidence was found.

I wished I could believe that would be the end, but I knew my death was the only way it stopped. I sighed as his broad chest met my back, and he pressed his lips just beneath my ear.

"Use your words."

"I don't know anything else. What happens if I need to run?"

"Then you'll adapt."

"I don't want to leave, you're here."

His hand came to rest on my opposite cheek and turned me to look at him. "Listen, your decisions can't be made because of me. In the end, it has to be what's best for you. And if leaving is best, that's what you'll do."

"You're telling me what I'm going to do."

"Chin up, my bratty boy. It'll work out like it's supposed to. Now, quit pouting and get to work."

I huffed and froze as the screen filled with a picture of Vernon. Perfectly groomed and wearing an expensive suit. Nothing about him screamed abuser or predator, who was suffering now that he didn't have me as a target?

"What's wrong?"

"He doesn't look like a monster. But I know how vicious he can be. Does he already have a replacement?"

"You can't worry about that. Right now, he's being watched too closely."

"He thinks he's above the law."

"How did you meet him?"

"A group of us were out at a club. I'd just gotten my first paycheck from my new job. My first job. He bought me a few drinks, and he seemed nice...attentive. I"—I cleared my throat —"I went home with him like I'd done with other men. It wasn't a big deal. I thought he was different as soon as he got me into his apartment, he wasn't just like all the others. The sex wasn't spectacular, it hurt, but it wasn't like the guys before. For a few months, I ignored the rough sex and was happy to feel safe, and he told me he loved me so easily."

I slammed my eyelids shut to block out his image on the screen, but it only intensified the hazy movie playing in my head. The visions were so strong that I expected to endure the pain again. All the humiliating details, some shameful enough I'd omitted them in court.

"Then one night we went out, and he wanted me to dance with someone else. I didn't see anything wrong with it, but later, he was mad that I seemed to enjoy it too much. He didn't even bother to use lube that night. The more I screamed for him to stop, the louder he laughed."

"He's a sexual sadist. It's about power and violence. He gets off on your pain."

"But what made me such an easy target? Do men just know I won't fight them?"

"Baby boy, if it wasn't you, it would've been another person he picked up in that bar."

"Intellectually I know that, but from past experience, I can't help thinking abusers see me as easy prey."

"As much as I want to make you feel better, no matter what pretty words I use, you still have to figure that out for yourself."

"Your Daddy voice is sucking today."

He laughed behind me and urged me off his lap as I hit print on a few more articles.

"I'm going to go pay for the copies, and we'll make contact with West and then kill some time until we go to the meet with Moffett."

I nodded as I sat back down on the hard-plastic chair and started signing out of the system. He'd told me that as soon as a session ended normally libraries purged search histories. I resisted the urge to check my social media accounts and my personal email. I closed everything and stood, slinging the strap of my messenger bag over my shoulder.

A smile curved my lips as I watched him talking to the lady behind the counter. I could see the interest in her eyes, but he didn't feed into it. Not even a casual flirting. I stayed back instead of approaching only because my face had made it onto the news more times than I liked. While my hair was longer and my face had filled out a little, I didn't see much difference in my appearance. Yuri was the type of guy that blended in and seemed comfortable in his skin—his place in the world. I was jealous of that.

When this was all over, I needed to think about how I wanted my life to go. New goals. I wanted to dig up those dreams I'd buried when I didn't think I was worthy of having them. He'd told me I needed to make my own decisions and find myself, but was it bad that I yearned to be better for him? It wasn't about the sex because other than kisses and that one-sided hand job neither of us had crossed any lines.

Every word he said to me was gentle and spoke of him caring about me. My life was off-kilter, but I wanted him. His Daddy voice. His lessons and correction, to have him claim me as his. I wanted to be better for myself, but why couldn't he be my reward? I shook my head and flipped my hood up as he turned to head back to me. Was my need gratitude or something more?

"IS THIS EVERYTHING?" Yuri asked as he lifted me onto a crate in a corner of a rundown warehouse space.

This was a little too mafia/spy movie for my liking, but Yuri seemed relaxed as he spoke to Moffett. My man turned and leaned back against the large shipping container and started flipping through the folder Moffett gave him.

"My guy said Vernon has taken a different man home every night. The investigator said he couldn't get anything out of them, but it appeared after he checked them out that they're into the rougher trade. Seems he's paying for what he can't get for free anymore."

I didn't look at what was in the file but tipped sideways to lay my cheek on Yuri's shoulder. He turned and kissed my forehead, then went back to turning the pages. There were more files and recordings to go through when we got back to the room. The amount of information we'd gotten from Moffett was overwhelming, or at least I thought it was. Yuri had taken it in stride and shoved everything into his backpack. We'd picked up Yuri's laptop to go through the flash drives.

"That won't satisfy him for long. Too much consent for him," Yuri stated without looking up.

"That's my thoughts. His old man is making regular visits to his penthouse, though. I threw some cash around. Vernon's drinking and drug use is at an all-time high."

When Vernon was high, his temper turned more violent, and I felt guilty he was taking the rage out on someone else. I didn't care if he was paying someone else to take it. Maybe they were like me, had no choice but to do what they needed to make a living. To have somewhere to sleep or a meal.

"Spiral?" Yuri asked.

"If I believe my gut, he's about to fuck up. Whether that's good or bad, I don't know. I doubt another victim will come forward."

That was my fear. That he'd never pay for what he did to me and the others we didn't know about. We'd discussed my survivor's guilt, and I agreed I needed to be able to get past it. That was easier said than done. Leaving another person to end up like me in Vernon's aftermath was unacceptable. Something needed to happen. He needed to be stopped.

"What about the case?" Yuri asked.

"As you already know, ten days until the judge issues a mistrial, unless they receive new evidence or Clarkson reappears, he's going to get off."

The deadline felt like a noose. And what could we do with so little time? I didn't want him to get away, but what power did I have?

"Could we set a trap? With his spiral and his need for violence, he won't be able to control himself."

"Something to think about, but you and your boyfriend are going to need to act fast."

I hid my grin against his shoulder as he didn't flinch when Moffett called me his boyfriend.

"Well, we have to come up with some sort of plan and soon. I can take all this?" he asked.

"Definitely. We'll meet up again in a few days and maybe come up with that plan. Back in my day, they would've just disappeared."

"Simpler times."

I covered my loud snort with a cough as I watched the two older men share a moment of camaraderie over simpler and more homicidal times.

"Back in y'alls days was the wheel invented yet?" I batted my lashes at them and earned two deep growls, but I loved Yuri's more. It made my stomach dance with nerves. I wanted to go back to our room.

"Man, you have to keep your boy in line. Petulant brat."

"One of his finer qualities."

"Another way of saying, you like giving him spankings."

"Okay, I'm hungry. I want food." I changed the subject and slid off the crate.

I shoved my hands in my pockets as Yuri put the new files in my messenger bag and handed it to me. The two men spoke a few minutes longer, and Moffett left.

"What do you want for dinner?"

"Anything?"

"Sure."

"I want sushi," I answered as he held out his hand and led me outside to the deserted street.

"I wished I could promise this would be over soon, but I can't."

"Yuri, I know that. I just want to get on with my life. This city is my home, and I don't want to have to leave because of him."

"But you'll do what's needed."

"I've been trying to escape for as long as I can remember. I'm finally feeling good about myself and my place."

That earned me another forehead kiss, and for some reason, I was addicted to those. In all my years, I'd never spent as much time with someone, and there wasn't intercourse or humiliation involved. Except for the whole on the run for our lives' thing, I wanted Yuri to keep me. I was trying to remember that he was just protecting me and showing me the treatment that I deserved.

I wanted sushi and chocolate, and copious amounts of alcohol and maybe lots and lots of anonymous sex. Okay, I wanted everything but that last one. Now if Yuri was offering the sex, I mentally groaned and focused on the stuff I could have, and it wasn't the sexy private investigator of my dreams.

NINETEEN

YURI

ONCE I FINISHED TACKING up the photos and notes on the wall, I stood back and folded my arms over my chest. Cross had to have fucked-up somewhere. I just wasn't finding it. Moffett was right—I should just take the kill shot and move on. I grinned to myself at the thought of putting one between Cross' eyes. That would settle the issue. Nothing could be done about the senior Cross but not every plan was foolproof.

The bathroom door opened, letting out steam and the scent of body wash. I turned my head to see Josh coming out with a towel around his hips and a smile curving his perfect lips. He drew near, and I uncrossed my arms and tugged him to my side. He hugged my waist. His skin was still damp where it met mine. I shouldn't have touched him that morning, but I wouldn't regret it.

If we'd met under different circumstances, he'd already be in my bed. We'd get there eventually. I wasn't letting my boy go. First though, we had some things to take care of and then he had to make decisions on his own.

"Love what you've done with the place."

"Well, it's either find a way to take them down without putting me behind bars for murder or you know, being responsible and finding a legal way to resolve the issue."

"Adulting totally sucks, but at your age, you should be used to it by now."

And there was my bratty boy. Some might see that as a turn-off but not me, especially when it came to him. Bratty meant he felt safe with me and that I'd succeeded with my plans. I should feel a lot more accomplished.

"I liked you better when you didn't talk."

He scoffed at me and smacked my stomach. "All your fault."

"Not my smartest move. But I'd prefer to be free."

"Kinda like you to stay free. Can't ogle you in jail."

"Nice to see you have priorities."

I gave him a tight squeeze and then pushed him to go get dressed.

"So, what are you looking at?"

He was moving around behind me, but even out of sight, I knew exactly what he was doing. In so short a time I'd learned to anticipate him and his needs. It had become second nature to do so.

"This is us trying to figure out how to get out of this situation without dying."

"Kinda figured that. What happens if I walk into court at the deadline and tell them what happened?"

"I'm more the proactive sort and not the sit around to wait kind."

"Then this must be driving you insane."

"It is, but in the end, I'd prefer you alive than with a bullet between your eyes."

"I'm all on board for that one."

"Cross is a spoiled rich boy, used to getting his way in everything, and his old man has enough money to throw it around. What I don't get is how this got to court." My eyes jumped from one item to another, trying to find some loophole, maybe something everyone was missing by looking at only the obvious things. Usually, the answer was in the minute details.

"The cops showed up for a domestic dispute by a neighbor having a smoke on the balcony below. They did their job when they showed, even if they seemed disgusted by the fact it was two men. District Attorney has delusions of grandeur and figured a high-profile win fast tracks him to the next level."

"So you didn't call the cops?"

"No, as you know, assault charges needed to be substantiated by the victim, but the loophole is if the incident is witnessed by responding officers. They heard Vernon's screams and busted down the door. Ambulance was called, and by the time I woke up, charges were filed, and the Feds were in my room."

"If you'd been awake, would you have gone along with it?" I already knew the answer to that before the question hung between us. He didn't know any different. His psychological evaluation hadn't given much hope that he'd live a normal life or experience healthy relationships. Before a certain age, children's brains were formed, and touch was a huge part of instilling a sense of safety.

He tended to self-soothe, hugging himself and rocking. I'd seen a documentary one night years ago while on a case, it was about orphans that were denied emotional and physical affection. They'd become emotionally and mentally stunted. A lot of them lacked empathy or the ability to distinguish right from wrong, but those were more severe cases. Some of them just simply failed to thrive—died from a lack of care. Starved for touch.

"Honestly, I think you already know what I would've done."

"But I want to hear you say it."

"I would've healed and let him continue to do it. When I was with him, death was my best-case scenario. I'm not saying I didn't see that everything about him and the relationship was wrong. I just didn't know any different. Did your mom think death was the only option?"

"I think so, but she was a product of an abusive cycle. Generations of women conditioned to be owned and abused. Mom dropped out of high school her junior year after my father knocked her up. He was a senior who just wanted a piece of ass, and Mom was conditioned to just go along with it."

"Is that why you're sympathetic to me because of her?"

I didn't want to be anything but honest with him. I turned away from my makeshift case board and found him sitting cross-legged on the side of the bed. I approached and crouched down in front of him. Folding my arms on his thighs.

"No, because of her, I wanted to do my job and move on."

"Then are you sorry you helped me?"

The misery in his voice broke me, and I hated that I hurt him, but it was safer for both of us if I didn't keep any secrets from him.

"Baby, I'm not sorry I helped. You've had enough people, especially men, lying to you over the years, and I won't be another one. It would've been safer if you ran. Let Arianna get you out of the country."

"I'm tired of looking over my shoulder. I want a life."

"I know you do, but we have to decide what's best and if that's letting Arianna make you disappear then that's what we'll do."

"I'm tired of people making decisions for me."

While I understood his point—his need for control—I couldn't let him die, not even to keep him around a little longer.

"Sometimes, we have to do what's right and smart. If we don't have this figured out, I'm calling in Arianna to get you out."

"You're not going to let me win, are you?"

He smiled as he laced our fingers, his skin soft and warm.

"No, I'm not. A new life won't hurt you. A place far away for you to build something better...with new choices."

"Yuri, I get what you're saying, but this city is all I know."

"We have ten days until the next court date. If we don't come up with more options by then, you'll call and have her people pick you up. Promise me you won't fight me on this."

We locked gazes, and he had no chance of winning in a battle of wills. As much as it pained me to think about sending him away, I'd known when we'd left the compound that this was one of the options. I was selfish. That didn't mean I couldn't think with my head and leave other parts of myself out of the right decision.

"I promise."

"Good boy. Now we need to work." I gave him a quick kiss, anything slower and I wouldn't be looking at the case the rest of the evening. I turned to sit on the floor, my back rested against the bed, my head on his leg, and his arms twined around my neck.

He sat his chin on the top of my head, and I could just about hear his thoughts. Every insecurity, his hate for being forced out, and I didn't disagree. He'd never had the chance to make a normal life. Almost since birth it was already outlined for him. Ever since we fled the hotel, I'd made sure to take his needs into consideration. Yet in this case, I had to go full Daddy on him and tell him what had to be done. We were forced to be together, but I didn't feel trapped by us.

The outside forces, the Cross family, they were the danger to this nice bubble of ours. What happened when we did succeed in ridding him of the threat?

I scrubbed my hands over my face, scratched my beard, and tried to free myself of the what-ifs. I was turning into an old, sappy fool, and his trust and gratitude was fucking with my head. Was I really thinking there could be something beyond this forced intimacy and that it could continue past the deadline of a court date? Why not?

TWENTY

JOSH

MY ANXIETY WAS at an all-time high as I paced our room and tried not to look at the papers and pictures lining the one wall. As Yuri had gone through paper files, and the ones on the flash drive, more print outs and handwritten notes joined the already overwhelming visual.

It was broken down into main players, Vernon and the Senator, associates in all ranks and some were just rumors. Looking at all of it brought back my days of sitting in court. I could still hear their voices. I wrung my hands as I walked the perimeter, stopping on each pass to draw fresh air into my lungs. The compulsion to self-harm began to ride me hard. A cold sweat broke out under my clothes, the cotton of my t-shirt sticking to the valley of my spine.

I was left alone for an hour. Yuri wanted to ask West a few questions and then was going to grab something for lunch and dinner. He'd tried to explain that he thought he recognized a few of the men from the surveillance photos. He was sure they were two of the men who carried out the hit at the hotel. I didn't remember anything from that day except the panic over losing Yuri.

He stilled carried himself a bit stiffly, but the two bullet holes were healed. The edges were ragged from where they'd had to dig out the rounds. He'd joked about not being as young as he used to be. Time wasn't erasing the memories of nearly losing him. I stopped and slowly pivoted.

Vernon Cross was the type of man men and women flocked to; they saw him as the ultimate prize. Rich and handsome, caring, but that was until you got to know him. A demon in the guise of an angel.

All I could think about was my past, and then when this was over, I was going to be forced to go ahead alone. Our previous conversation came to mind. I needed to prepare for the separation. I'd become addicted to not just my emotional attachment but the strangeness of the sexual attraction. It was abnormal territory. I'd never experienced it before. While I found men sexy before, with Yuri, I wanted to do more than look—to fantasize. I just didn't see it happening, even though I'd allowed him to cross the line.

What the hell had I been thinking when I let him get me off? Since then, it was all I was thinking about. I wanted one night before this was over. I wanted to forget everything that was on the wall. Every man I let use me for a moment of belonging.

He was too controlled to break, no matter what I did. We shared a shower, a bed, and countless kisses, then the one release where he didn't demand me reciprocate.

I heard his special knock, and then the door was opening, I held my breath as he entered the room. The sheer mass of his body seemed to make the space seem too small. His hands were loaded with bags, and I rushed forward to take them, but he waved me off.

"Grab some cups, baby."

"Okay."

I hurried to the bathroom to grab some of the heavy plastic cups that he'd picked up. He'd picked us up some plates and silverware too since we'd planned to be locked down for a while. When I entered the main room, he was laying out subs and fries on the desk in the corner. I smiled as he placed lunchmeat and cheese into our cooler packed with fresh ice.

"I know you're probably sick of sandwiches. Once this is over, I'll get you whatever you want."

"And as I said, I've never been picky about food. Three meals a day, snacks and all stuff I like too."

It wasn't as common as before, but I still found myself waiting for him to tell me when to stop eating. He was strict about candy and my lethal levels of caffeine, but other than that, he didn't try to control me with food.

"What has you skittish?" he asked as he placed my food on a plate. The sub was cut into three pieces like I preferred. I snarled as he handed the sandwich, fries, and carton of milk to me. "You'll drink it. Then you can have your soda."

"Yes, sir." I pouted to make him smile.

"Now, answer my question."

"The wall. Looking at him made me remember. I wanted to hurt myself." He removed the items from my hands and placed them back on the desk.

"Do you need correction?"

The fact he asked me was a surprise. I remembered feeling lighter after the last one.

"Bend over the bed and place your hands on the mattress." There was the order. The decision was taken from me, and I approached the bed, shoving my pants over my backside. I waited, nerves twisting my stomach, and I flinched as his left hand spread over my lower back. His thumb was teasing the top of my crease. I was hyperaware of the hair that I hadn't waxed since the hospital, and it made me self-conscious.

"There's no shame in telling me you need guidance. If you need correction for your unhealthy thoughts, then that is something Daddy does for you. You'll get ten only. Each one you'll count and tell me why you're being punished."

"Yes, Daddy." I fisted my hands in the comforter, and I wasn't prepared for the strength of the first smack. I yelped and tried to get away.

"Unless you count, Daddy starts over at one."

"One. I thought about hurting myself."

Each strike filled my eyes with tears until they fell to the fabric covering the bed. I counted and repeated why I was getting my spanking. But with each admission, fire flared in my cheeks, and there was such a strange comfort that my body didn't respond to the agony. It was as if my brain no longer craved the pain.

Once I reached ten, he helped me straighten and kissed the tears from my lashes and cheeks.

"I want you to go wash your face, and then you'll have dinner."

"Yes, Daddy. Thank you."

He brushed his lips to mine, and then I quickly went to wash my face so I could retrieve my dinner. When I entered the room, he was back at the desk.

"I'm sorry. I know having to look at everything hurts you. My brain works better if it's laid out for me or working in a noisy bar."

"Bar?"

"Yep, I always find the sleaziest neighborhood bar and set up shop in a booth or at the bar."

I huffed and sat on the end of the bed and crossed my legs. I gasped as the burning built and no way I adjusted eased the pain. I stayed silent as he pulled the chair over and sat down in front of me. He patted my thigh.

"Tell me why you thought about hurting yourself."

"It reminded me of my stupidity and horrible decision making. Going home with him that first night just seemed like any other one-off I picked up. He seemed different, though. Cultured and polite, he even opened the back door of the limo for me. He didn't paw at me or grab my crotch. I fell so easily for it." I let out a bitter laugh as I picked at my food. "I can't believe I actually bought the *we can just talk* line he threw out."

"He was a born manipulator, baby boy."

I almost protested when he took my plate and his, setting them on the bed. He picked me up and cuddled me on his lap.

"Doesn't change that he was in a long line of manipulators who saw me as an easy target."

"Is it different now? Would you recognize them for what they are?"

If I was supposed to concentrate, this wasn't the way to accomplish that. He was rubbing my thigh through my sleep pants and higher to stroke his thumb across my belly, his hand slipping beneath the cotton.

"I don't know, and if you want me to think, that's not the way to help."

"I'm sorry my boy finds me so distracting."

"That's another thing. You can't keep saying mine." I stared at him from under my lashes. My focus as always falling to his mouth. Plenty of men had kissed or tried to in the past, but it was all a part of the plan to get me to bend over. It didn't mean more than a cold seduction—a cruel means to an end.

"Why not? It's probably stupid on both our parts, but one day when this is over, I'm hoping when you've had time to think and find yourself that you'll come back."

"Really?"

"Yes."

He lifted his hand to my cheek, and he touched his lips to mine. It was chaste as if he wanted nothing more than to comfort me.

"I'm not going to make promises or lie to you. When this is over, I probably won't look so attractive, but once we have some distance and the adrenaline or whatever has faded, maybe you'll want to come back."

"You're not going to fuck me, are you?" Disappointment and elation were a mix I'd never experienced. As I said I wanted one night, but it was intoxicating he wouldn't use me as a toy.

"No, don't mistake my gentlemanly attitude. It isn't easy for me at all. Getting you off yesterday morning made it so much worse to rein myself in."

"But you didn't let me repay—"

"No, you don't owe me anything. Just because I jacked that pretty cock of yours doesn't mean you have to touch me in return. I don't require that from you."

"What if I want to?"

"Not until we're out of this fucked-up place and I have you in my bed. Privacy and hours of freedom."

I stuck out my bottom lip, and I gasped as he sharply nipped it with his teeth. As his fingers fisted in my hair, he controlled me and turned my head however he wanted me. The kiss was a promise of ownership but not the kind that stripped me of my bodily autonomy. I knew all I had to do was say no and he'd stop; no matter how heated our exchanges became, he'd never force me.

Our groans mingled as the kiss turned deeper, and he showed me his strength as he lifted me to straddle his thick thighs. I rocked my hips and felt the thick ridge of his erection behind the zipper of his jeans. I hugged his neck as my head fell back, and he gently sucked at the length of my throat. My gasps turned loud and high-pitched. All panic and worry were gone, I was free, and the need for pain receded until it was as if it hadn't existed.

He was shoving his free hand between our bodies. I caught his wrist and lifted my head to rest my forehead on his. I tried to catch my breath.

"No, if I can't touch you, I don't want to."

His breathing was ragged and he trembled, his thighs flexing under my ass. It pained me to make him stop, but I couldn't handle another one-sided orgasm. I wanted more.

"Very well. Now, it's time for you to eat. Your lunch is an hour late."

"You're not mad?"

"Baby boy, no, I'm not mad. I will always take your needs and feelings as priorities. And when and not if I claim you, we're going to do it right."

"Yes, Daddy."

I smirked as he groaned, and his fingertips bit painfully into my hips. I was still aroused and wanted to get off, but I'd rather go without if I couldn't make him feel as good as he did me. The Daddy was a low blow though. As put-together as he seemed to be, that title did make him lose some of his steely control. He gave me another quick kiss then settled me back on the bed and gave me my plate back.

For the next three hours, he told me in detail about his talk with West and that we'd be moving to another location the next day. I was going to miss the outdated motel room and the gaudy wallpaper and bedspread. The shaggy crimson carpet. What I hated the most was we weren't going to be alone. Moffett and West would join us.

Would he change how he treated me? Maybe I wouldn't get

the kisses and cuddles when others were around. In some ways that broke me, but it also showed that our time was coming to an end. A definite plan would be put into place to either free me to live my life in the city I considered home or an unknown place with a new name and life. A life without my grumpy Daddy.

TWENTY-ONE

YURI

AS I SECURED Josh's bulletproof vest, I watched the happy light slowly dim. I'd visited the storage unit to grab us both one. The longer I was with him, the more I just wanted to pack up and have Arianna make both of us disappear. Morally I couldn't do that. Cross needed to be stopped so that he couldn't repeat what he'd done to my boy. I tightened the last strap. I tried not to think about this being our last day together.

After our last kiss and I told him I wasn't going to have sex with him or in his words, fuck him, I'd noticed a distance forming. Two mornings of awaking and finding him on his side of the bed; I hadn't realized how accustomed I'd become to sharing a bed with him. I'd turned on my side and dragged him to the center of the bed. Unconsciously, he snuggled into the curve of my body seeking my warmth.

"I don't like this." He ran his hands over his chest and stomach.

"And I understand, but we're going to be with West, and I want you protected if something goes down."

"Why are we going with him if you don't trust him?"

I knew he didn't understand why we were moving. Even

as I explained it, the plan didn't work for me either. Josh needed to be free, and in order to do that, we needed to get rid of the threat. One way or another, I was going to do just that.

"Right now, the only person I trust is you. And as the saying goes, the devil I know if better than the one I don't."

"We're safe here."

"But for how long? We can't hide out here forever, and I want someone with you. The next week is critical, and I have places I need to go that I won't take you. You remember the plan?"

"If the new safehouse is compromised, I'm to call Arianna."

"Exactly. I'll make contact as soon as I can."

He turned away from me, and I fisted my hands to keep from grabbing him. Most of the morning he'd kept himself busy unpacking and repacking our bag, folding each item ten times or more. I'd allowed him to have time to think while I dismantled my suspect wall.

I had a long list of names and places to visit in the next few days as we prepared to carry out our plan. If we couldn't take them down in court, then I would have to sink to their level. Although, blackmail was a dangerous game. It could go nuclear at any time. I had to keep our enemies on their toes just long enough to arrange a meeting with the judge.

Walking Josh into the courthouse on a deadline had its own set of problems. Judge Callister was known as a strict but fair judge. Had a reputation above reproach. Moffett couldn't find anything on him. Not even one corruption rumor stained his record in his thirty years on the bench.

I needed to think over my options. Yet, I also had to make sure my boy was safe in my absence. It galled me to have to rely on West again. He didn't have any direct blood on his hands, but he also hadn't thought twice about turning away for enough pay.

West was a crooked bastard, but he'd never fucked me over personally. And I hoped he didn't start now.

A knock rattled the door. As I drew my weapon, Josh ran until he was pressed to my back.

"Stay behind me, if something goes down, you run while I distract them." I didn't wait for an answer. He'd do what he had to.

I crossed the room, drew a deep breath in through my nose, and exhaled as I turned the doorknob. Opening the door just enough to see through the crack, West stood on the other side. Wordlessly he pushed it open and stepped into the room.

"You ready to go? I found a safehouse. Damn place looks hours away from being condemned, but you can't be too picky."

"I thought I told you to wait outside?" Why I expected him to do anything I said, I had no idea, but I holstered my weapon and slammed the door he left open.

"Um, have you seen this neighborhood? I was in warzones more hospitable. Where's our witness?"

I turned my head to glance down as Josh peeked around me to wave at West.

"Damn, when did he get so pretty?"

When West winked at him, a growl slipped out, and my hand flexed around my gun. My former partner was known as a ladies' man, but I'd seen him take home a pretty boy or two over the years when the urge struck him. For the most part, West was one of those slick, sickeningly handsome men who could easily get a bed partner. He wasn't getting my boy, though.

"I knew it. You always had a weakness for the pretty, submissive ones, Sorenson."

"Yeah, yeah, whatever, let's get on the move. I want Josh settled with dinner before I have to take care of a few things."

"I'll go out first, Josh will be behind me, and you bring up the rear. I'm sure you can handle that."

I rolled my eyes as I made my way to our bag, slung it over my shoulder, and when I turned, Josh was right there. I raised my hand to pinch his chin.

"Baby boy, you'll be fine. Have I broken my promise yet?"

He only shook his head. I shot a look at West to find him watching us. I didn't give a fuck about his judgment and turned my focus back to my boy. As I tilted his head up, I lowered my mouth to his. It was a comforting act. We'd have plenty of time for more later. Or at least I hoped so. When I straightened, he wrapped his arms around me, and I hugged him for a few minutes until I couldn't put off leaving any longer.

"You stay close to West. Now, go put your hoodie on."

He did as I said, and I mentally prepared for the exit from the motel. I had to clear my head and remember I had a job to do. Taking care of my boy was my top priority.

We quickly outlined the plan, West got into position, and I gave my boy's hand a quick squeeze to reassure him. West and I both drew our weapons, and then years of working together took over. The moves seamlessly in sync as we stepped into the hall. It was still early enough in the day there wouldn't be any real activity until the ladies started to bring back their tricks for the night.

The fire exit I'd checked when we arrived and noted it was broken wouldn't draw any attention by sounding an alarm. I rested my free hand on Josh's shoulder to prepare to pull him behind me if needed. A feeling of wrongness tingled at the base of my skull, but I ignored it as we descended the stairs, checking each floor as we did and then we were moving to the hidden door under the steps. We paused, and I turned my upper body to check for any danger.

Still clear but I held my breath as I glanced at West to find him easing the heavy metal door open. The hinges creaked, and my nose snarled up at the rotting stench of a dumpster the motel shared with the restaurant next door. West pushed, then he quickly checked our blind spots.

"Come on," West said then the beep of the car alarm signaled him unlocking it.

He kept it running and had only taken the fob with him. Everything was too easy. We'd stayed hidden too long. My paranoia amped up as I quickly got my boy in the backseat and West jogged around to the driver's side. I shifted until I could throw our bag inside and then I was closing us in, ordering Josh into the floorboard until we were sure no one followed us. A hit team would've taken us out as soon as we appeared from the exit.

Still, I couldn't relax. In our room, it was easy to hide from the world—to pretend that all was normal. Josh hugged my calf and laid his head on my knee, while I soothingly combed my fingers through his silky hair. I kept my attention on the move, checking behind us as we drove away from the alley. West would take a few false turns to make sure we didn't have a tail, but after that, it was to the second location.

A few more days and hopefully this would be over, but until then, I'd do everything to keep my boy safe and unharmed.

A FEW HOURS LATER, the sun was beginning to set. The house we'd entered should've been condemned before. You could look through the rotting downstairs ceiling to the rooms above. West had prepared the place as much as possible. Sleeping bags. Lanterns and other camping equipment. There was a construction sign out front. West said that it was an old friend and they ran crews late there, so it wouldn't cause any alarm.

I had to laugh at the murderous glares Josh was sending West. My boy wasn't happy, and it showed. I was about to suggest him not sleep around Josh but figured at least he was occupied.

"Do you have to go?" he whispered, as he rested his forehead on my chest.

He was always touching me in one way or another, but since we'd left with West, he'd sought more comfort. I'd ignored West clearing his throat whenever my boy curled up on my lap. Whatever he needed, I was going to give him without question.

"Yes, I have to meet up with Moffett, and then we got a few people to see. You'll be fine with West. If you do kill him, make sure to keep his gun."

"Yes, sir."

"One way or another, this will be over in a week. Either we'll keep you hidden until you walk into court before they declare a mistrial or—" He kissed me to cut me off.

"I don't want to think about leaving."

"Josh, just because we don't talk or think about it doesn't mean it's not going to happen. You have to be ready."

"I'll deal with it when it's time."

I let it go. I didn't want to argue before I left. I wanted to make sure he was calm while I was gone. Procrastinating wasn't an option, so I gave him a quick kiss, made sure West was set, and I left by way of the back door.

It wasn't a neighborhood to be walking around after dark without causing suspicion. I was armed, and while normally my identification and concealed carry permit would get me out of trouble, I still didn't know if they had a *Be-On-the-Lookout* issued for me. I was to meet Moffett on the other side of the city. There was a bus stop a few blocks away.

THREE TRANSFERS and a few blocks later, I walked into a dark Jazz club. Soft music played from a jukebox in the corner.

A few men were seated at the bar, and I looked around until I spotted Moffett in a back booth. He had an open laptop and several files spread out on the tabletop. He was tapping an empty rocks glass beside his computer.

"What can I get ya, hun?"

The bartender called out as I passed, and I ordered a double bourbon neat, and whatever Moffett was having. She nodded, and I continued until I could slide onto the bench seat across from him. His steel-gray hair was sticking up in all directions, and his eyes were glassy from lack of sleep or too much alcohol, maybe both.

"I was wondering if you were showing up." He didn't look up as he picked up a manila envelope and tossed it in front of me.

"What's this?"

"If we can't get the younger Cross, we can make his old man squirm a bit." He stopped talking when the bartender stopped beside the booth. "Put it on my tab, sweetie."

"You going to finally pay that tab or get me fired?"

"Don't I always make it worth your while?"

"If you're talking about that exciting five minutes including foreplay, I'll take cash or credit when you're done here."

"Ouch, hit a man where it hurts."

I chuckled as she flipped him off and disappeared. I bent the clasp up and then opened the flap. The stacks of pictures I pulled out were definitely not going to do Senator Cross' Presidential run any favors. I flipped through the images, and each one showed the younger Cross in a compromising position with about a dozen different men, three in the same photo.

"I think Cross knows what a bastard his son is."

"What he doesn't know is half those boys are underage. Street kids. Vernon appears to have a habit of finding boys on the street and then doing whatever he wants with them. I got my hands on a few medical reports..." He pointed at the stack. "Those are included. Those are just since the trial started. I dig deeper, and I'm sure I can find more.

"How much of an exclusive would I get if I said the God-fearing Senator isn't above getting a blowjob when a pretty boy is ready and willing to kneel?"

That would change everything. Rumors started to come to light when I started to dig that said the Senator had bailed his son out several times to keep his company going. Vernon was going through his profits quicker than he was making them. Sooner rather than later, bankruptcy was going to be Vernon's only out—or jail for embezzlement from his company. Some cushy Federal Prison was too good for the bastard. I wanted him in General Population of a State Institute. "You have evidence?" I took a sip of my drink and waited for him to answer.

"Maybe...what do I get?"

"What do you want?"

"I'm in need of a new investigator...pro bono."

I was expecting a steeper price, but that was yet to be seen. "You got it."

He tossed me another envelope. The image was grainy as if taken from a distance from a cheap camera and through opened blinds. The man was insane, but you'd think a Senator living a double life would make smarter moves.

"Cross is going down fast. His drug use is out of control, and his violence is increasing. I don't think he's got anything to do with trying to take out your boy. The Senator is pulling the shots on this one. Although I don't think the Senator knows just how deep of shit his son is in. Cross owes a few shady people quite a bit of money for fronted drugs."

"They're both making some fucked-up decisions."

"True, but if you get rid of Cross' backup by getting the Senator to back away and stop all assistance, he has no one to run to. On the outside Cross is protected by his name and standing, inside he's fair game to any organization he owes money to. Right now, he's got all the aces in the deck. Doesn't mean we can't make his old man scared enough to force distance between them."

"How would you play it?" I knew what I'd do, courier service and a letter to Senator Cross, with a possible meet.

"Not a lot of options for you in this. Getting near him is going to be a nightmare. We can go for an old favorite, have a letter delivered and arrange a meet. Right now, you and Josh are dead men as soon as you show y'all's faces. It might be an idiotic move, but time is quickly running out."

"Wasn't too far off what I was thinking. We need to move fast. You got another copy of this?"

"Several. I haven't made many friends in my business. I always keep backups."

"I'll send this tomorrow morning."

"I'll keep an ear out, but I have another thing for you."

"What's that?"

"I went through all the names you gave me; your friend, West, made for interesting reading. Seems he's under investigation for witness tampering and destroying evidence. They put him on desk duty about the same time your hotel was hit. My informant says he was trying to destroy a high-profile case."

That tightness and tingling was back at the base of my skull. I'd trusted him, and now he was fucking me over again. He was also alone with my boy. I demanded Moffett's keys and the location of his vehicle. My heart was beating its way out of my chest. I barely remembered grabbing the information he brought me or running from the bar. All I cared about was getting across the city. I could deal with my ex-partner betraying me, but when it came to putting my boy in harm's way, that was something I was going to make West pay for.

TWENTY-TWO

JOSH

I TRIED NOT to touch anything as I paced the lower floor of the construction zone. The no-tell-motel seemed healthier. Daddy had left a weapon in case I needed it and I wondered if I could hit a mutant rat when it came for my throat. I checked the time on the antique pocket watch he'd given me for luck. He'd told me it was the one thing he had left from his childhood. His mom had passed it down to him on his sixteenth birthday and said it had belonged to his grandfather.

He'd told me a lot about his life. Things he said he'd never shared with anyone. I was the only one who knew about his mother and father, and that life had been good when his father hadn't come around. Happiness filled the stories he'd shared, but he also shared the horror of seeing his mom lose herself as soon as the bastard decided to show up. I sympathized with his mother. There was a need to be wanted even if it was just to be used as an object.

She was the reason he took the protection job. He sought atonement for a sin that wasn't his. He believed that if he saved at least one person that it would make up for not saving her. Decades of guilt weighed him down, but I'd seen a different side of him after the hotel—a caring and nurturing man, a gentle Dominant—a Daddy.

I'd learned a lot about myself in such a short time. I'd had well-meaning people offer advice and guidance before and after Vernon, none of it had meant anything until him. He showed me what I deserved in the way he spoiled and touched me. Our futures were perilous at best. Yet for the first time in my life, I felt hopeful that everything would work out. Maybe that was naïve, but I didn't care.

I wanted to hold tightly to it while I could. Although, the pessimistic part of my brain wondered if I was addicted to him as much as I was the pain. I tried to remind myself about the difference between abuse and correction. I'd handled my natural submissiveness as if it were a flaw. Even if Yuri and I parted ways when this was all over, he'd given me the example of what I needed. That didn't mean I wasn't hoping his talk of a possible future wouldn't come true.

A floorboard creaking drew my attention to West entering the main room. Comfortable wasn't a word I'd use about how I felt in his presence. He put me on edge like a predator. I'd spent most of my life as prey sensing danger. Instead of running, I froze. He wasn't a large man. Tall and slender, a bit too good-looking, the type of looks that made you self-conscious just by existing.

"How did you wrap Sorenson around your little finger, huh?" He was staring at me with his arms crossed over his chest.

His gaze moved over me from top to bottom, then back to my face. I resisted my natural urge to retreat.

"What do you mean?"

"In the years I've known him, he's never let a piece of ass control him."

"We haven't done anything." My voice quavered as I mentally thought of my escape options. Yuri had walked me around the house and showed me the best ways to get out fast. He even made me up a *go-bag* with phone, money, and a change of clothes.

"Now, why don't I believe that?" he asked as he took a few steps. "The kisses. The sitting on his lap. And you're not too particular about who you bend over for."

He closed the distance until he was within touching range and that's when I did retreat.

"Yuri won't like you talking to me like that."

"I'm not going to tell him about getting a blowjob from his pretty, little boy."

I bent my arm behind me, flipped open the strap, and I heard the pop of the button securing the revolver in the holster. I was told not to pull it unless I was willing to use it. Fear choked me as he reached for me and I pulled the weapon. My heart was beating too fast, and the weight of the gun was awkward. I curled my finger around the trigger, took a deep breath, and started to tell him to back off when the windows at the front of the house exploded.

"Down," West yelled, and I hit the floor.

I nearly dropped my gun as I was crawling across the floor. Adrenaline taking over as I grabbed my bag and shoved the weapon inside. I kicked at West as he seized my ankle and I fought my way across the rough, hardwood planks. Chunks of drywall and thick dust filled the air as more rounds tore at the walls.

He was saying something to me, but all I could think of was to run like I was told. A loud grunt sounded when I looked back to take aim at his nose. When I connected, he covered his face with both hands, and I took my opening. When I reached the kitchen, my brain cleared, and I stared at the backdoor. Were there more men waiting out back? Were the shots through the front windows just a ploy to make it easier for them to catch me?

I was confused, but Yuri told me to run. *Think, Josh, think,* I screamed at myself. I suddenly remembered the break in the side fence. The dining room window was close enough to the ground I could jump. Briefly I darted a glance into the main room to find West returning fire. Maybe he wasn't one of the men trying to kill me, but I wasn't taking any chances.

I yelped as I surged to my feet and a shot hit too close to my head. I felt the nausea building. The terror threatening to take my legs from me, but I ran to the other room. I cursed as I fought the sticking window until it opened enough for me to slip my small frame through. I stuck my head out, and no one took a shot, so I jumped out and squeezed through two off-set fence boards.

I swear I could feel my heartbeat in my head as I stayed low. Dogs barked, and I heard sirens in the distance. I didn't trust anyone but Yuri, and I wasn't taking the chance of waiting on him from the shadows. I moved through yards, the people starting to fill the sidewalks to gawk at the police presence, and as quickly as chaos reigned, everything went quiet. I slung my backpack onto my shoulder, flipped up my hood, and made my way through the night hoping to find a payphone.

I couldn't use the cell. No one answered if it wasn't an assigned location with a familiar number. My legs shook as I checked the address and realized a bus station was nearby. I could find a phone there to use. Bus stations were typically pick up points. There were always people around. Vehicles dropping off and picking up, I'd make my call and wait there. I didn't want to leave Yuri, but I promised I would take care of myself first. He'd know where I went. He had the numbers and codes too.

All I knew was that I was tired, my hands were beginning to shake as the adrenaline wore off, and I was in need of some lethal amounts of caffeine to ease the crash. I didn't want to worry about West. Maybe he was in on it, maybe he wasn't, but I wasn't sticking around the find out.

The walk was longer than I anticipated, and I swung my bag around to dig out some money for caffeine and break it for some quarters to make my call. I darted into a convenience store, grabbed what I needed, including a few snacks and candy bars to hold me over for a while.

Should I go back? Yuri hadn't left long ago. He told me not to expect him until late, but I could hide in the bushes until he returned. I instantly vetoed the idea. I didn't want to break the rules, and if the cops were still there when he arrived, he'd leave. Me going to Arianna's was the only option. At least Yuri could call and make sure I was there.

I walked into the cavernous building and voices echoed, the wheels on luggage clacked over the grouted seams of the flooring. I quickly found the bank of payphones and checked the receiver before pressing it to my ear. I inserted a few quarters and dialed the number. A clipped voice answered, and I gave them the code for the location. They told me to wait outside in twenty minutes and hung up. I found an uncomfortable wooden bench and sat down. I bounced my legs up and down on my toes. My nervous energy was increasing as I took inventory of my surroundings.

It was an overwhelming symphony of annoyed grumbling and a baby crying. People glanced around, but everyone avoided eye contact to stave off unwanted attention or conversation. Was West dead or was he one of the people setting me up? My thoughts were a frenetic stream of what-ifs and second-guessing. I'd followed the rules, and all I could hope was I didn't have to wait long to hear Yuri's fate.

I checked the time and got up to head outside. The night air was cool, and fall would be coming soon. Even after years off the streets, my brain calculated how much time I had to find a sanctuary for winter. The best soup kitchens. The safest abandoned buildings or shelters, one year I'd spent the whole of the freezing weather at the compound.

I stepped out of the shadows as a familiar van with a star painted just below the side mirror pulled up to the curb and the passenger door opened. I ran and jumped in as fast as I could, the man behind the wheel was unfamiliar, but the symbol on the van showed me I was safe. We didn't share any conversation as we made our way through the evening traffic and out of the city. The closer we got, the more the adrenaline high eased. I ate a candy bar and chugged a double of canned espresso, then another.

Usually, we'd wear a blindfold, but I'd always known the location of the compound. I just respected the rules. The gate creaked as it opened and as soon as we parked, Arianna appeared from the front door.

"Yuri called. I told him we had you."

"Is he okay?"

"Yes, he just has to take care of a few things, and then he'll call for a pick-up. Let's get you inside. Have you eaten?"

"Candy bar and coffee."

"Not ideal and Yuri made sure to order me to feed you."

I sank into Arianna's arms as she wrapped me in them, and for the first time since the bullets started, I let it go. She half guided and half-carried me inside the house. Yuri would be there soon, and until then I was safe. I could only hope he stayed the same.

TWENTY-THREE

YURI

I WAS SEETHING as I waited outside the emergency room waiting for West to appear. I'd seen the paramedics loading him into an ambulance. He was bitching the entire time that it was only a flesh wound. Federal agents and cops had questioned him for nearly an hour before they'd allowed him to be treated with more than a bandage. He'd lied to me for the last fucking time.

It wasn't as if I'd completely trusted him, but he'd done some pretty shady shit over the time we'd worked together, and I'd gotten caught up in it after the fact. He loved his job, took pride in it but now he'd gone too far. I'd tried to give him the benefit of the doubt. A case like Cross' could quickly move you up the chain of command.

All I could be thankful for was Josh being safe. I'd found the nearest phone after I'd arrived and seen the house surrounded, lights flashing and everyone in the neighborhood checking out the excitement. When I'd heard the click, I'd demanded to speak to Arianna. It took three tries before they'd put her on. All I asked was did she have him? When she'd said yes, I said I'd call later for a pick-up. I knew it wasn't protocol, but I didn't give a fuck when it came to my boy. The call wasn't long enough to cause issues for anyone. I'd be there soon enough, but first I had to take care of West and setting up a meeting with Cross.

I resisted the urge to meet up with Vernon and take care of ridding the world of him myself. No one would mourn him. Just one less sick, rich fuck to prey on innocent people. I kept checking my watch and then the door. Each minute that passed was another notch my rage and frustration rose. West would sign himself out against doctor's orders if needed. If I knew one thing about the bastard, he hated hospitals and doctors.

All I wanted to know was what went down. My boy wasn't an option to ask. I also had several more questions for my former partner to answer. He'd planted evidence a time or two, but he never tampered with witnesses. Hell, he pocketed the occasional loose cash, but I hadn't thought him capable of attempted murder or an accessory to one. I hadn't had any choice but to bring him in. I couldn't have found the information I needed at the local library or through the Information of Freedom Act, especially on an open case.

I needed to scope out the courthouse and other buildings to see what security was like in the records departments. Usually, if you looked like you were supposed to be there, no one said much.

Finally, he appeared and was standing out front messing with his phone. Probably ordering a car to pick him up. I rushed out of the darkness.

"You scared the fuck out of me. What the hell are you doing?"

I didn't answer except to press the barrel of my gun into his ribs. "Don't make a fucking sound, we're going to take a ride, and if you lie, I'll pull the trigger with no regret."

He opened his mouth but closed it fast when I dug deeper into his side and led him across the street to the parking garage where I'd stowed my SUV. I secured his wrists and ankles with zip cuffs, then tossed him in the back seat. Thankfully he wasn't struggling or yelling for me to let him go. Even if he did, it wasn't happening. We had several things to get straight, and then I needed to get to the courier office. Sunrise was approaching, and by the time I was done, they should be open.

I carefully wove my way through traffic to my storage unit. I pulled up to the gate and punched in the security code, the fence slowly opened, and I drove through. I'd asked for a unit at the back of the lot. I parked, jumped out, and unlocked it. Then I lifted the door.

Quickly I got my vehicle inside and shut us in. I kept the lights on but cut the engine.

"Man, I can explain."

"You better be able to, I have plenty of questions."

I threw him to the cement floor, and bright beams had him covering his eyes.

"I don't know where Josh is."

"Oh, I know. Fortunately, I know where he is. I got some intel that you were put on desk duty for tampering with a witness. If they had enough evidence, you'd be disgraced and running back to the parents' mansion. What the fuck is going on?"

"Okay, when the Cross case landed on my desk, we were called in to take care of witness interviews. As high-profile as the case was, the prosecutors wanted to bring us in to handle witness location. Clarkson was already on board for the trial."

"So you took the money?"

"No, someone a lot higher on the food chain did. I was already on the hook for it because I was one reprimand from losing my job, at the worst going to jail. We were told to ignore anything that made Josh look credible. In the end, he was the only witness, and I quickly realized that someone ordered a hit on him. After a few close calls and suspicious activities going on around the safehouse, I came to you."

I wasn't surprised by any of it. Too much revolved around politics. Exchanging of favors for future help or funding, a vote on a new law. If the Cross case hadn't appeared so high-profile, it would've been another.

"Keep going. I'm still debating whether to shoot you or not. A dirty agent turning up in a few weeks floating in the harbor won't make too many waves. Especially you, your friends are almost none."

"I may be a bastard who's controlled by his dick, but Josh is a good kid. I took one look at the file and hospital records and knew if he didn't kill Josh, the next one to fall at Cross' feet wouldn't be so lucky. So I protected the only witness, but then the defense came forward with one witness after another claiming to have at one time fucked him. They were willing to get on the stand to swear he liked to be roughed up."

"And then his testimony would be completely discredited?"

"Exactly, but the Senator and his son weren't satisfied with just a not guilty. They wanted Josh completely out of the way. I was as careful as I could be, but I think they hid a GPS on my car or were just following me. Different teams to make sure I didn't get wind of it."

"Why should I believe you and not dump your ass in the harbor after putting a round between your eyes?"

"You're not a killer."

"No one fucked with someone that belongs to me before."

"There is that." He bent his knees to place his feet flat on the floor but left his arms lowered.

I noticed his usually perfect tan was sallow and he had dark circles under his eyes. His features pulled with the strain of his injury. I didn't feel any remorse for grabbing him outside the hospital. Dirty or not, I couldn't see him getting his hands bloody being too close to a murder.

"Do you have names?" I paced the width of the unit, one side to the other, I repeated the path trying to work out the details, what would help, and what wouldn't. Less than a week and we'd walk back into the same courtroom. The deadline was too close with more to do.

"None that will do you any good. When I showed up at the hotel to try to scare him off with the defense's character witnesses, they must have followed me inside and checked which floor I got off on. Easy enough to ask the staff about a boy as pretty as Josh."

"If you want to remain living, you'd do well to stop telling me how pretty you think my boy is."

"I did tell him that he had you by the balls."

I wouldn't deny it but I sure as hell wasn't admitting it out loud. "We're not changing the subject."

"I'll do whatever, I tried to fix it and only fucked-up."

I didn't trust him and probably never would, but his usual modus operandi was he leaned toward being cocky about his abilities to get away with anything. Bragging wasn't beneath him. He'd talked plenty about the women he'd fucked while on the job, from witnesses to witness family members. As long as I'd known him, he was ruled by his dick.

"You think the same hit team was responsible?"

"I don't know, but I can guess that they'd have something to prove. They did go excessive. Maybe to make sure the job was done. How did Josh know how to get out?"

"We talked exit strategy as soon as we got to the safehouse, just like I did with every place we stayed or visited. I packed him a *go-bag* for him to grab. I also armed him."

"I know, he shoved that gun in my damn face seconds before the front windows exploded."

"And why would he pull a weapon on you?" My boy hated carrying the gun. I'd heard him complain enough. What the fuck had West done to provoke him that badly?

"He took my joke a little too seriously."

"And the joke?"

"Nothing important." He was looking everywhere but at me. I knew he'd shoved his foot in his mouth in that inappropriate way he had.

"I'm still up in the air about shooting you. You might not want to piss me off by not answering my questions."

"Then, I might not want to answer your question."

"I should leave you here to starve to death." I stopped my frustrated pacing and leaned back against the grill of my SUV. I scrubbed a hand over my face and beard, I was tired, and my new fucked-up shoulder ached like a bitch. What I needed was a nice long vacation without wet-work teams or crazy exes.

"You could, but decomp would smell up your things. You know you can never get that smell out."

"I don't like or trust you. When this is over, I don't want to see you again, are we clear?"

"Crystal. I really didn't mean to set him up."

"But you knew it was going to happen."

"True and if it makes you feel any better, when this case is over, I'm history. They may call it something else, but I'm getting fired at any minute."

"Good. You don't deserve the badge you carried." I removed a knife from my pocket and tossed it to him. "If you want to be helpful, you hear anything useful, make sure I hear about it."

He cut through the ties at his ankles easily but struggled with the one around his wrists. I wasn't offering to help.

"I'll message you. I'm sorry, Sorenson. This job is all I got. I can't lose it, and when the boss says to let a few things slide and my latest reprimands would disappear, I didn't have a choice."

"You always have a choice, West. Your ego and wallet nearly got an innocent man killed."

"He's different though, man, he didn't back down. He kept his shit together. The Josh I met wouldn't have done that."

"Just get out, I have shit to do, and then I have to get back to him."

I would've rather killed him, but I let him walk out. Knowing my boy was safe with Arianna wasn't the same as seeing it for myself. I dug out a few things of mine and Josh's, shoved them in my pack. The envelope addressed to the Senator was stowed inside as well. I'd mail it and call for a ride. I was too old for this shit, but I had a job to do. At least I knew that in a week this would all be over. Both of us needed to move past this.

West would fuck himself over sooner rather than later. Maiming him while it would have made me extremely happy, nothing would make him learn. I checked my watch, and I still had an hour before the store opened. Maybe coffee and breakfast to kill time because sleeping wasn't going to happen until I was with Josh.

TWENTY-FOUR

JOSH

THE PERFECT DREAM didn't exist until that moment. The tickle of Daddy's rough beard on the side of my neck. The way he easily lifted me from my cot in one of the communal sleeping rooms. "Come on, baby boy, I can't sleep without you." His voice was a gruff whisper in my ear, and I felt weightless, gently rocked by his pace through the house and up the stairs. A door slammed somewhere in the distance, but I forced myself to stay asleep.

My body sank into a too-soft mattress, my clothes were stripped, and I moaned Daddy as his weight settled between my thighs. His hairy body was perfect on top of mine. I searched blindly for his mouth but it didn't take too long because his lips found mine. The softness of his belly rubbed my hard dick.

"Daddy." I rutted against him as I felt the bump of his cock head against my hole. He nipped at my lips, traced them with the tip of his tongue.

"Wake up, baby boy." He nuzzled the side of my neck.

"I don't wanna, you'll be gone."

"Fuck, baby boy, I've tried to be good...give you time." I felt my dream Daddy start to retreat, and I frantically clutched at him to

keep his weight on me. "Calm, shh. Daddy's going to take care of you."

"Yes," I hissed as he straightened and spread my legs wider. I wanted this to be real. To have him loving on me like I'd fantasized about since our first kiss. But I needed something...this wasn't perfect. Yet, it was all I could ask for.

With his hands behind my knees, he pushed them back to my chest, and I took over, holding myself wide. I held my breath in anticipation. Kept my eyes squeezed shut to stay in the dream. I didn't want to wake up and be on my cot alone, still unsure if he was safe.

My nails dug into my skin as he lubed me inside and out, and I felt my cock jerk. His movements were fast yet gentle as he stretched me just enough.

"I need you to wake up."

The thick head of his dick pushed to my opening, and I whimpered. It was all too much. The section of my brain waiting for pleasure to morph into fear pushed into the dream.

"Only good boys who listen to their Daddy get what they want. You'll open your eyes now."

Sadness became a suffocating band around my chest as I opened my eyes. A gasp slipped out as he didn't disappear. The rough plane of his hand stroked over my belly, across my chest, and teased my nipples.

"There's my beautiful boy. Do you want this? Use your words."

The pressure of the fat head of his cock increased as he nudged my hole.

"Yes, Daddy, please."

The feral grin that transformed his face was nothing like the gentleman of before. Danger and contentment became a maelstrom of conflicting emotions. Just as I was going to reach for him, a scream tore from my throat as he took me with one brutal thrust.

I bit into my lip, and I grabbed his sides. His gaze was locked on mine. I felt the weight of him, his warmth, and the coarseness of his body hair. His hips were slapping against my ass with each slam. When I clenched around him, a growl teased my mouth.

I was equal parts loved and used; discomfort eased into something more. I lifted my head to watch his thickness stretching my hole wide. The metal frame of the single bed banged against the wall. I lifted my arms and wrapped my hands around the bars.

He braced himself on either side of my head—his fists sinking into the thin pillow. I arched my hips to meet the downward movements of his. I felt every thick inch. I wanted more. I wanted harder. My tongue wouldn't work to form the words, and tears stung my eyes. I wanted to beg, but I'd never been an active participant. I was a body to come in and nothing more.

"I'm not gonna last, baby boy." His mouth captured mine and his hips sped up, and then he was jacking my cock in time with his thrusts. The pads of his fingers and palm were rough against my sensitive shaft. Pleasure and pain combined into an experience I had never come close to achieving before.

I stilled with my hips tilted in the air—every muscle in my body pulled tight as I waited for something. It was strange and terrifying, and then a long moan slipped from my lips to his mouth. Come covered my belly, and I jerked my hips higher, then his full weight collapsed on me as he ground against me. I held on to make sure he didn't leave me, but all he did was roll his hips upward, and he slipped free.

I didn't like the emptiness. He rolled us carefully until I was sprawled on top of him. Our harsh breathing filling the quiet. More mornings than I could count—this is the way I awakened.

Him already awake and stroking his fingertips along my spine. It was safe and familiar, this was ours, something special for us, and he didn't complain I was too heavy or it was too hot. While there wasn't much difference in our heights, I'd sworn he'd grow tired of me doing that at some point.

"I told Arianna that I was stealing you from the communal sleeping room. I searched for an empty room. I didn't think they'd appreciate me attacking you on your cot."

"We wouldn't be the first. I thought we weren't going to do this?"

"Probably wasn't my best idea, but when I came back to the house to find you gone, all the worst-case scenarios played out in my head."

I wasn't hurt, but the adrenaline crash earlier had made me feel lost and vulnerable. I'd only fallen asleep because of exhaustion. We'd both needed to know the other was okay. I wouldn't deny I wanted a lot of repeats, but I also knew on an intellectual level that when the danger was gone, I'd need to reassess my life. And sex was a huge factor in clouding my judgment, especially sex with him. "I vote for you waking me up like this every day. And before you say it, I need to take my time and think."

"I'm sorry."

I lifted my head and crossed my arms on his chest, then laid my chin on my forearms. "What are you sorry about?"

"A lot of things. I left you alone with that bastard West. You almost got killed...again. I can keep going."

"It won't always be like this. One day we'll have nice, boring lives."

"Oh, with you, I don't think life would ever be boring. We need a shower. This time you'll be naked in there with me, and I won't be weak from blood loss."

I eased off the bed. "I'll get the water started." I ran for the bathroom, feeling lighter than I had in forever. I bent over to turn the water on. When I straightened, I had a big, solid man pressed fully to my back. I slightly tilted my head as he sucked at my neck, but not hard enough to leave a mark. His rough hands stroked from my chest to my groin, and then across the top of my thighs.

After he helped me into the shower, we took turns washing between kisses. Not much was said after that. Once we dried off and returned to bed, he flipped down the covers. He laid down first, and I draped my naked body over his. I pulled the covers over us and inhaled the scent of his skin. I missed his body wash and cologne.

"What do we do next?"

"A few more days we'll have a meeting with the Senator. Moffett helped me find some intel he doesn't want to get out. Taking him out of the equation leaves his son without financial backing. It seems he's only holding onto his business and social standing because of who his father is. Without him, Vernon loses everything."

I rubbed my cheek on his chest. The deadline on whatever this was we had was quickly coming to an end. Walking away, even for a short time, was going to kill me. I'd always felt trapped in the past, and even when we were in hiding, I'd felt freer than I ever had before. He'd made everything right with the way he cared. Even when he had all the opportunities to take advantage to use me for a quick fuck with no expectations, he hadn't done that until today, and that was only a way to assure each other we were alive.

"What happens after court?"

"We'll discuss that when it happens. Right now, I want to sleep with you."

That only softened the blow. We both knew that when I walked out of court, he'd send me back to Arianna. She'd already arranged for me to receive counseling when I returned. Someone to talk to who would help me get better on my own. If he saw that I wasn't using him as a crutch, that this was more than one moment and a memory to fade in time, he'd worry less about thinking he didn't give me choices.

I closed my eyes and listened to the steady thump of his heart; I didn't think I'd fall back to sleep but knew he needed his rest. I drew circles on his chest. Savored the soreness and relaxation of just being. No one could find us there. It was a sanctuary for at least a few more days. I knew I should feel relieved that it was all coming to an end, but while I was ready to be safe, I didn't want to say goodbye.

TWENTY-FIVE

YURI

ARIANNA SET me up with an attorney that looked like he was a mob enforcer. I felt like I'd have to sell my soul to avoid ending up at the bottom of the harbor. Dominic Kluge was at least three inches taller than me and outweighed me by a good hundred pounds of muscle. She'd assured me that no one fucked with him and he didn't care who the fuck he was going against. He was currently sipping espresso from a tiny cup and appearing bored from the other side of the table.

I kept checking my watch and was still a half-hour away from the meeting time. I'd chosen a busy cafe in the middle of the day. Kluge had agreed to take care of anything to do with Josh. I didn't have a ton of stuff or money, but what I had would go to him in the event something happened. I'd had my Will drawn up that morning, and Kluge would sell everything and give the proceeds to my boy to give him some cushion to start a new life somewhere.

My plans were kept between me, Arianna, and Kluge. I didn't want to get my boy thinking I was planning ahead in the event I died to make sure he was happy. My last connection to anyone was my mom, and when she was gone, I had nothing and no one left, but Josh had quickly become mine.

I couldn't believe only a few days earlier I'd loved on him for the first time. Since then, we'd talked and shared kisses because we both knew anything could go wrong. All the bullets we'd dodged was proof of that.

"Do you think he'll show?"

"If I was him, and I had secrets that would destroy my chances to run the country, I'd want to make sure they never saw the light of day."

I hoped so, after this we were out of options and except for making sure Josh made it to testify, then disappear. I'd calculated all the options and what was best. That was all I could do.

The bell over the door signaled someone entering, and I turned my head to watch as the Senator entered. He appeared to be alone, but I didn't trust that. He probably left his security detail outside. His gaze moved around the room, and when it stopped on me, I saw the recognition on his face. It was in the way his jaw tensed, and his movements were stiff. He was an older man with gray hair and a suit that probably cost more than I had in my bank account.

"Mr. Sorenson, I presume?"

"I see you've done your research."

"You were thorough as well."

I motioned to the extra chair I'd pulled up to the table for him. A server approached the table and asked the new arrival what he wanted. He waved her off.

"Since I'm here, let's get this over with. What do you want from me?"

Kluge took another sip of his coffee and placed the cup on the saucer. "I'm representing Mr. Sorenson and Mr. Clarkson. It has come to my and my associates' attention that you, your son, and parties unknown have made physical threats against my clients. In light of recent events, we for the time being, respectfully request that you remove all financial backing from Mr. Vernon Cross effective immediately."

"You want me to hang my son out to dry over a piece—"

"Senator, I'd be more careful about your statements about my clients. I cannot advise Mr. Sorenson to release the information he's acquired, but I have it on good authority that the papers would be clamoring over it. Can you imagine the headlines, Senator caught with underage sex workers and male ones at that?"

Kluge's voice carried, and the Senator turned white as he frantically darted his gaze to the nearby tables.

"Can you see your approval ratings? Especially among your conservative supporters. The Evangelists alone line your pockets to push through discriminatory legislation. Your biggest fundraiser was organized by the vastest religious organization in the country."

"Can't help your son is on trial for trying to kill his male lover," I said as the color kept draining from his face. Sweat started to darken the blue of his dress shirt. "You remove all support for him, let him face his charges, and you'll be lauded as a hero. Disowning the sinner and letting him suffer the way he deserves. A clean break, a nice press conference demonizing him and making yourself look like the good, god-fearing man that you are."

If it was possible, I'd allow them both to go down. He was a hypocrite, but his son was a violent man who wouldn't stop. If it wasn't Josh, then it would be someone else. He was already repeating his behavior on men he'd picked up. It was only a matter of time before someone wasn't as lucky as my boy and turned up dead. The first kill was always the hardest, but with repetition and practice, it would become easier. Vernon was a narcissistic sociopath, and his violence would only escalate, especially with his addictions.

"We all know that without your support, he has nothing. His business, *your* former company, is only a few months from bankruptcy, and then they find out he's been using his employees' money to live the lifestyle which he's accustomed to."

"Which scandal would you rather have? The one that shows you in a good light for denouncing him or the one that will make your chances for presidency non-existent?"

He sat there looking sicker by the second, and I knew his answer, but was as much a sociopath as his son was, the thought of giving in enraged him. I didn't give a fuck as long as my boy was okay.

"Listen, I don't give a fuck about you or your son. You can do what you want with him. But if you don't do what I want, every image I have of you and your son's activities will go to every news outlet in the country by tonight. Make your choice now, because as soon as we walk out that door, I'm going through with my promise. I assure you I don't make empty threats when it comes to Josh's safety."

Long minutes passed as his jaw clenched and relaxed at regular intervals. It was killing him, but he knew what he had to do. He just didn't want to admit that he'd lost this one. He was a man who'd always gotten what he wanted. Born with money he'd and made more over his lifetime, he was in a position of power. And that was being threatened.

"What assurances do I have you won't release the information you have even after I do as you ask?"

"You don't. First sign of you backing out, whether that's tomorrow or ten years from now, I'll make sure you pay."

"Within the hour, Vernon won't have attorneys or financial means." He surged to his feet and left without another word.

"I was hoping for a bit more strong-arming if I'm honest."

I chuckled at Kluge's disappointment. "Are you really an attorney?"

"I wasn't always one. I had other...interests and sometimes still do."

"I'm sure. Do I owe you anything?"

Arianna said she'd called in a favor to an old friend, but I liked to pay my own debts.

"As a private investigator, I may have need of your services in the future."

"You know how to contact me. Well, I better get back to Josh. I'm sure he's worrying himself wondering how everything went."

"Sorenson, not many people would go toe to toe with a Senator over some pretty thing, why?"

"To be honest, I hadn't planned to at first. All I wanted was to get back to my life after a job was done, but I had to make sure he was okay."

"Even if that's without you?"

"Yes."

"Very noble. I don't meet many men like you. Go comfort your boy, and I'm going to enjoy another espresso, and the handsome barista making them."

I grinned as I darted a glance to the counter to find a tall, slender man, maybe in his mid to late twenties. Tattooed and heavily pierced. "Enjoy." I stood and headed for the door.

I'd anticipated some sort of relief with the Senator's agreement, but it wasn't there yet. Maybe when we walked into court to find the army of lawyers missing or saw a press conference. I'd never been the trusting sort. Letting people in was harder for me until Josh. I had few if any friends. That didn't mean I didn't want to take a chance with him. We both had work to do, him more so than me. Although, I'd give him all the time he needed.

"I was wondering how long you'd be."

Arianna's voice surprised me, and I found her leaning back against a van.

"What are you doing here?"

"Figured you'd need a ride back to the compound. How did it go?"

"For right now, he agreed to the terms. Won't trust him until I see it. It's good you showed up, I need to speak to you privately."

I didn't hide the fact that I wanted him to go back to her to have time to think. My need to make sure he was okay in every way from mentally to physically was a natural compulsion for me. I wanted him in my bed and life, but it was more important to me he learned healthy coping mechanisms. While I'd helped to a point, there was a time when professional intervention was needed.

"You want to make sure I'll take Josh in and get him help. I already said I would."

"Okay, maybe we don't need to talk."

"Sorenson, you might be a bastard on occasion, but you care for Josh. That's more than he's had before and you want to make sure he's mentally and emotionally ready to start a normal life that has nothing to do with pain and abuse. After court, I'll take him. I already talked with a therapist friend who agreed to see him as a favor to me. I want to thank you for not taking advantage of his vulnerability."

"My mom was very much like Josh. She just didn't survive the last beating."

"He'll do just fine. I've never seen him as happy as he's been since he met you. When he brought you to us to save, I saw how broken up he was, and that emotion had nothing to do with dependency on another man. You showed him he was worthy of care even if he wasn't on his back for you."

"I hope so. I tried to be noble."

"Your restraint ended with denting my damn wall. Next time, find a room not next to mine."

I snorted as she rolled her eyes and pushed away from the van to get into the driver's seat. I jogged around and got in. We didn't talk much more than idle conversation on the way back to the compound. My head was too busy with thoughts that soon I'd have to watch him walk away and I wondered if I was strong enough to do so.

TWENTY-SIX

JOSH

I WAS BARELY HOLDING down my breakfast as I walked into the courtroom looking more confident than I felt. Yuri had slowly bathed me in a tub filled with bubbles and dressed me in a suit that was a few sizes larger and better fitting than my last one. My new attorney was on one side and Yuri on the other. For long moments that morning, I'd fought off multiple panic attacks and telling Yuri I wasn't going. His *Daddy* voice wasn't even working on me. I tried to take comfort in his presence and lap time, but all I could think about was if I'd survive the day.

Yuri had taken care of Senator Cross. A little blackmail and an allegedly mob-connected lawyer went a long way. As long as certain photos weren't released, Vernon lost all support from his father. Which meant there went his army of high-priced representation. But I knew how dangerous he could be when he didn't get his way. I wore the marks of his cruelty.

The prosecutor approached me and came up short as he looked at Kluge and Yuri.

"Mr. Clarkson, you've caused quite a few issues."

"There wouldn't have been issues if you'd provided adequate protection for my client. I made the call that he remained underground until court reconvened. If it wasn't for Mr. Sorenson going above and beyond in his duty to keep Josh safe, you wouldn't have a witness at all."

"Of-of course, have a seat up front, and once the formalities are out of the way, we'll call you to the stand to finish your testimony. It appears Mr. Cross has had to change attorneys at the last minute, but that won't affect your role. As of right now, with everything that's happened, we're asking he be remanded to custody or put on house arrest until sentencing."

All I could do was nod. I darted a glance at the defense side and found Vernon sitting with a single lawyer in a poorly made suit. He was whispering to Vernon, and his face turned redder, again the rage he directed at me when our eyes met made me take a step back.

"I'm right here, baby boy. He's not going to get to you."

I wanted that move where he pinched my chin to make me focus on him and his words. Yet that wasn't possible. I had to be an adult when all I wanted to do was be little and have him take care of me. In this, I needed to stand on my own feet and just be honest, no matter what was thrown at me. I wasn't proud of my past, but I also wasn't ashamed of it.

I'd used sex because it was my only currency. Between having a full belly and a warm bed or freezing to death, I suffered through the few minutes of fucking. It was something that meant nothing to either of us. With Vernon, it was my first real attraction, someone I could see building a life with, but then I learned what he was. By then it was already too late to escape. I was isolated and without friends, held hostage because I was financially imprisoned.

Too many stayed in abusive relationships because their partners controlled the money. First, they take your friends and family, neither of which I felt I had. Desperation breeds insecurity, which turns into a dynamic of dependency. Even if the first hit had never happened, he would've never let me go.

I slowly made my way down the aisle, and I sat, leaving enough room for the men on either side of me. Yuri crowded me and placed his arm over the back of the seat. I glanced at him to find him staring at me with affection in his gaze as he gently massaged the back of my neck. He knew his touch calmed me, and until court was called to order, he'd soothe me in whatever way he could.

That's what I was addicted to the most, the way he made everything okay. That's why I wasn't going to argue when it was time to leave. I wanted to come back whole and ready, with no doubts on either of our parts.

The judge entered, and the bailiff ordered everyone to stand. I watched the beginning of the preceding with only half my attention. I could only stare at the witness box and realized I was going to have to face both sides.

"Is the prosecution ready to call their witness?"

"Yes, your honor, we call Joshua Clarkson."

"You got this, baby boy. Just keep your eyes on me."

I nodded as I stood and made my way to the stand. I felt all eyes on me. No cameras were allowed in the courtroom, but reporters lined the back rows taking notes for the news. I'm sure they'd have something to say about the change in attorneys and my sudden reappearance. My quiet, anonymous life turned into a circus—a headline for the morning edition.

"Mr. Clarkson, due to circumstances that resulted in attempts on your life, we're going to refresh the jury about your last appearance here in this courtroom. The defendant, Mr. Cross, claims that your supposed abuse was a result of consensual rough sex. Is that true?"

I took a deep breath, let my gaze connect with Yuri's, and told my story again. I didn't pay attention to the judge, jury, or

Vernon. I answered questions fired at me from both the prosecution and defense. Hours of sometimes repeating myself. Even asked if I could be treated as a hostile witness, but through it all, I kept my eyes on Yuri. He gave me encouraging smiles when I stuttered. All that mattered was him and my testimony. Today it ended. After this, I took my life back and forged a new path.

I WAS MENTALLY and physically exhausted as I exited the courthouse. The judge remanded Vernon to jail until sentencing after evidence came to light that he'd attempted to kill a witness. He'd been warned that charges may be filed for that as well. I said bye to everyone but Yuri and walked into his open arms.

"Freedom, how does it feel?"

"I'll see after I experience it a few more days and nothing explodes around me."

"Josh—"

Whatever he was about to say ended when Arianna appeared beside us. She was dressed in a conservative pantsuit with her hair in a matronly bun. It was odd to see her outside her hippie clothes or her jeans and t-shirts.

"Are you ready?" she asked.

"No, but I guess it's about time. Could you give me a minute?"

"Sure, take all the time you need." She gave us both a sympathetic smile and backed several feet away to wait.

"Do I have to go?"

"Baby boy, you know it's for the best, but it's not forever. Arianna is going to get you some help, and when you're strong and ready, you know where to find me."

"What if I can't sleep at night?"

"We'll be in the same boat then. Before you, I've never shared a bed with anyone."

I rubbed the silk of his tie between my fingers and studied the striped pattern. He looked handsome in a suit, but I was kind of partial to him in his jeans and hoodies or even better, shirtless.

"Every day Monday through Friday, I'll be in my office. Being a good Dominant means I have to take care of you even if I don't like it. You need to learn your own path. I've only given you the basic skills. I don't care if it's a month from now or a year...I'll be waiting."

I felt the warm, wet trail of tears falling down my cheeks. I angrily tried to wipe them away, but they only came faster.

"Hey, don't do that. I'm going to miss you, too."

He pinched my chin, and the all too familiar move did its job of commanding my focus.

"Your office?"

"Yep, and if something changes, I'll get a message to Arianna with where you can find me. I'm not leaving the city if it isn't with you."

"What if I don't need you after?"

"Then you don't need me. We made no promises for forever. All I ask is you come to say goodbye."

"That I can do."

"You better go. I'm sure she's ready to get back home. I'll be waiting." He gave me the softest kiss, and then he was backing away.

I bit my tongue to keep from calling him back as he pivoted on his toes and descended the stone steps. Just as I was about to say fuck it and run after him, Arianna circled my waist.

"If he said he'd wait, he'll wait. He's an amazing man who wants what's best for you, and that is the sign that it'll be a healthy relationship."

"What if he finds someone else...better? Someone who doesn't need time to figure out his fucked-up head?"

"I don't think he'd do that without talking to you in person first. He made a promise to you."

I watched him until he crossed the street and disappeared into the parking garage. This wasn't him running to the store or going to track down a lead, and then he'd come back to our room. No, he was going to drive off, and I didn't know if or when I'd be ready to go to him.

I let her lead me in the opposite direction to where I knew she'd parked her vehicle away from the courthouse and prying eyes. The farther I got away, the heavier my body seemed to be. I knew it was for the best, so did he, but I wished my heart agreed.

TWENTY-SEVEN

YURI

I'LL BE WAITING. That's the last thing I'd said to him as I'd let him go. Arianna was waiting to take him away. I knew it was for the best, but that hadn't made the decision to let him go any easier. A lot had happened since he'd arrived in my office weeks ago. As much as I wanted to believe it was real, we both needed some time apart to analyze our feelings for each other without the cloud of danger weighing us down and forcing us together.

A week had passed, and sleep was in short supply. I found a house to rent, and possibly buy if I decided to settle in. It was a nice place to make a home. My savings and the money West paid me for my time would keep me going until I could get my business off the ground. I could deal with cheating spouses and missing person cases, less excitement didn't sound like a bad thing.

At least that's what I kept telling myself when what I was really doing was just biding my time until my boy came back. All I had was an agreed-upon weekly email to tell me if my boy was okay. No details just a *he's okay*. I didn't want to influence him or myself. Part of me didn't care how we met or if the situation made us see something that wasn't there; all I knew was I wanted him. I needed it to be his choice when he was ready to make it. We weren't reciting vows or promising forever, but I wanted a beginning.

A knock sounded at the door, and I yelled for whoever to come in. I wasn't doing well dwelling in my own thoughts. The door swung open, and I groaned. I started to reach under my desk to where my gun was in the holster I attached to the underside.

"No need to start shooting," West said with a snort, and proceeded to make himself at home.

"What the hell are you doing here?" We weren't very friendly, but in the past, I hadn't wanted to shoot him as badly as I did now. Especially since he tried to proposition my boy in that half-assed, crass way of his.

"I'm bored since they fired me and I have plenty of time on my hands."

"I'm sure you could find better things than bothering me."

He seemed to think it over. "Nope."

I ignored him and started going through the messages I'd gotten the night before. It wasn't anything too exciting, but busy work never hurt anyone.

"When are you going to forgive me? I didn't fuck you over. I just followed orders. And if it's the other thing, all I did was ask your boy to get on his knees, and that was a joke."

"We don't joke about you hitting on a boy I own."

"You own him now? Where is he then?"

"I sent him away to think."

"You were always so noble. What if he finds a less grumpy and considerably more handsome Daddy?"

A deep rumble filled my chest, and I hated someone hitting me below the belt by throwing my own worries in my face. I knew I wasn't the perfect option. Josh was a lot younger, and damn my boy was beautiful, but he had his choice. I'd made sure he had the tools to make wiser decisions when it came to men. I showed him how he should be treated and loved on, and that he didn't need pain. That's all I'd wanted for him, but then my feelings changed, and he became irresistible.

"If that's what he needs, all I want is him to be happy."

"Come on, man, fight for at least one of them. Playtime is all well and good with a temporary fuck, but this one had you by the balls. You're going to give that up for his happiness?"

I knew he didn't get it. He was selfish and manipulative. Sex was nothing more than getting his dick wet then getting out. He had the emotional depth of a sewage-filled puddle. I didn't need to justify anything to him.

"Yeah, why not? He's had enough bastards manipulating and abusing him. I won't gaslight him and force him to come home. When he's ready and sure, he'll come back, or he'll have a nice life with a different set of priorities."

"I swear, sometimes I don't get you." He shook his head and lifted his right leg to rest his ankle on his knee.

"The last woman you fucked was the barely legal daughter of one of your witnesses."

"She was twenty-five, and she just wanted to fuck. We both had an understanding. Inappropriate or not, mutual orgasms were all we wanted."

"And I think there's more than getting off. We'll agree to disagree."

"Oh please, tell me the last person you fucked before Josh? You probably can't even remember their name. Just because you're smoother about it doesn't make it any different."

He got me there. I'd never gone beyond dinner and one night. If that made me an asshole, I'd accept that. But if I didn't see myself going on date number two, what the hell was the point in drawing it out until the other party got hurt? Maybe I should've put in more effort, but I didn't see the point.

"It makes it plenty different, at least I find my pool of fuck partners off the job." I clenched my jaw as he raised a brow and smirked. "Okay, before Josh. But I'm sure you didn't come around to talk about my possibly non-existent relationship. What do you truly want?"

"I need a job."

"Oh no, that's not happening."

"Come on, Yuri, you know I'm a trust fund kid. But dammit, asking my grandfather for it would mean a nine-to-five corporate job. I can't do it. He'd put me in the mailroom to *work* my way up just to fuck with me."

"Does it look like I'm overwhelmed with jobs?"

"Moffett is throwing your name around. I hear you got an in with a connected attorney." He pointed at the slips of paper in my hand. "And that's a stack of people wanting to hire you. I'll work cheap. I have some savings."

"I'm surprised the bureau hasn't seized your accounts yet."

He snorted. "Like I'd keep that money in my accounts."

"One day you're going to push your luck too far, and someone is going to shoot you."

"You haven't yet, and I've fucked you over pretty badly."

I went through the messages and found a cheating spouse one and tossed it his way. Outlined pricing and expenses, all the things that would pay my bills, but another thought hit me. "Don't fuck the client."

"But what if—"

"Don't. Fuck. The. Client." I enunciated each word to make it clear. "You don't fuck up that job, and we'll talk about it."

"An audition, really? I've been your partner for years, and you're going to do me like this?" He waved around the slip, and I chuckled at the horror on his face.

"Yes, an audition. If everything works out, we'll see about using you on occasion."

"Yeah, yeah, whatever you say, you're just trying to get me to leave so you can obsess over your boy."

"No, I just want to get rid of you. Don't mess up that job. Word of mouth makes or breaks a business, and I don't want you thinking with your little head and put me out of business."

I really did want to get rid of him. It was coming up on the end of the day, and I was going to hit Vices for a drink before heading home. He looked like a chastised two-year-old as he stomped out of my office and slammed the door behind him.

I wasn't looking forward to going home. I was sleeping on a thrift store couch in a sleeping bag. I needed to do something. If my boy came home, I had to at least have it ready for him. That meant doing up the guest room too. I wanted him to have a choice if he wanted to be in my bed or do the whole dating thing since we hadn't had the traditional start.

Shit, I needed to stop thinking about him, or I wouldn't make it. I had to remember this was my idea. I removed my weapon from under the desk and slid it into the holster at the small of my back. I concealed it with my t-shirt and grabbed my backpack. With my keys in hand, I left my office and jogged to the street below and walked right into the club.

"Sorenson, you're early today." Kiki, the regular bartender stood tall behind the bar, and it had nothing to do with her six-inch heels.

"Just starting out...not much to keep me busy."

"Your usual?"

"Yes, thanks."

"Not a problem."

She poured me a double of top-shelf bourbon, and she winked as she heavy poured. Her life hadn't dimmed her happiness yet. She was recently divorced and going back to school to finish her degree. She said dancing made her the money, but it was also a way for her to decompress when life was too heavy.

She set my drink in front of me and then left me alone to enjoy it.

The music didn't drown out my thoughts or worries. I was forty-five and starting over, but all I wanted was Josh to come back. And that was something out of my control.

TWENTY-EIGHT

JOSH

I GOT out of the car in front of Glittering Vices and stood there, tipping my head back to look toward the third floor where his office was. I was unsure about being there. Weeks had passed since we'd parted ways at the courthouse, and all those earliest insecurities about us tried to play out in my head. I knew he would've come to me to tell me that what he felt was a mistake. He'd have shown me that much respect, but every day, I'd waited.

Vernon was sentenced to ten years and went on trial for the additional attempts against Yuri, West, and myself. He wasn't going to see the outside anytime soon. Without his Senator daddy's help, he wasn't doing well in his little cell fending for himself. He wasn't exactly up to taking on the other prisoners, and that didn't bother me in the least. Knowing he was learning what it was to be defenseless and without choices made the years I'd spent with him worth it. I'd put him away, and he couldn't hurt anyone else. I only regretted that the Senator hadn't shared the same fate. Although, that was the way the world worked. That was all over now, and it was time for me to start building my life—the life I deserved.

With a deep breath, I took the first step, and the next, each one I told myself he would be happy to see me. I grinned as I took the *Help Wanted* sign where it was taped on the heavy door and entered the building. I jogged up the stairs to the offices above the strip club and stopped when I reached his door. The age-etched glass had his name stenciled on it. This was it. I lifted my arm and knocked, wondering if I was about to make a fool of myself.

"Come in." Yuri's gruff voice easily traveled through the office door, and I was nervous. I'd spent a month at the compound and going to a therapist three times a week. At first, I'd been hurt when he'd told me I needed to find myself, and when I was ready, I could find him. Arianna had ridden my ass the whole time I was there. Without his influence, I'd started to spiral downward a bit. The confusion became almost more than I could handle.

That's when I'd made a decision and the reason I was standing outside his office. I wanted my Daddy back. And in the end, I understood that he wanted me to make the decision for me and no one else. I'd decided he was the best for me.

I opened the door and smiled to find him sitting behind his desk, his reading glasses on, and he looked sexy as hell. I'd missed him. I leaned my shoulder on the door frame.

"Hello, sir, is the job still open?" I held the help wanted sign between my hands.

He raised his hand and removed his glasses, and then he relaxed back into his desk chair. He carelessly tossed his glasses on the desk, and that stare I remembered seemed to see right through me. I hadn't said a word, but I felt as if all my secrets and failings were on display.

"Do you think you're qualified?"

"I don't know. What are my responsibilities? I'm a quick learner, and I'm not averse to some stern correction."

"Is that right? Do you feel you'll need a lot of correction?"

"Oh yes, I try to be good but sometimes—"

I couldn't help smiling as his laugh slowly built.

"Took you long enough, baby boy."

"Been interviewing other boys to take my position?"

"Lined up around the block to my house."

"Is that right?"

"Yeah, wore this old man out."

I knew he was joking, but my jealousy took over, and I gave an unimpressive growl.

"Get your ass over here," he ordered, and patted his desk. He pushed his chair back to open the space in front of him.

I inhaled one more time and walked into his office, closing the door behind me. Before I could go to him, he held up his hand.

"Lock it."

Swallowing hard, I turned the deadbolt and tossed the sign on an empty desk to the right of the door. I cautiously approached, still fearful of what would happen in those next few minutes. While I felt more comfortable in my skin, I'd lost some of the confidence and safety he'd fostered in me in our time together. Sometimes it seemed like a lifetime together, but I knew we'd only spent a month trying to stay alive.

What if he'd changed his mind about me being his boy? That I'd romanticized my Dominant—my Daddy. Things could still so easily get mixed up in my head. I circled around his desk and sat down on the edge, scooting back until my legs were dangling.

"Use your words, baby boy."

"I want to come home."

"And where is home?"

"You are." I saw him readying a protest, but I spoke before he had a chance. "I've been seeing a shrink three times a week since

I went back to the compound. My head isn't perfect. I still get confused. I wonder if all my progress will collapse in a single blink. I'm not fixed, and who knows if I ever will be. You told me to take my time and think. To decide what's best for me without pressure or expectation."

"And what did you decide?"

"I want you. Those first few weeks I thought maybe I'd made you into the Prince Charming that swept in to save me."

"And now?"

"Still want you, but I'm scared to death."

"It's okay to be scared. To not know what the hell you're doing. I sure as fuck don't."

"That's encouraging." I rolled my eyes but froze as he moved his chair forward and pushed my thighs open.

"Josh, all I've had is my job. I'm still working on what to do with the rest of my life. So we can deal with what comes next together. It won't be perfect, but we both know this is going to take work. I've never done long-term, and you're going to keep going to therapy. A month isn't long enough to heal everything. In some cases, it's something people need to work on for years."

"I know, and the therapist has an office in the city, and I already set up a weekly appointment."

"Where's your things?"

"In my motel room."

"Why didn't you bring them?"

"I didn't want to presume that I'd be going home with you."

"Silly boy. Now that you're here, this is what you're going to do..."

He had his left arm around my waist and grabbed a pen and pad with his right hand. He scribbled onto the paper. "This is my address. You're going to go to your motel, check out and go home. You'll start work here Monday, but until then, you'll settle into the house."

"You're not coming with me?"

"No, I have to drop off a few files to finish up a couple cases. You have a few hours to decide if you're going to be settled into my room or the guest room."

"You don't want me in your bed."

He growled as he slipped his hand up to fist in my hair and brought my mouth down on his. I whimpered as it all rushed back. How I loved the tease of his beard. The roughness of his hands as he controlled me. The heat and passion of our one and only morning, loved and fucked in equal measures. I'd thought about it many times after realizing how lonely a bed was without him. Sharing a bed with him had spoiled me in the weeks we'd hid out in our cheap motel room.

"Fuck, baby boy, you stayed away too long." His voice was gruff as he spoke between kisses—his tongue teasing mine. I rubbed my hard dick against his stomach as his fingertips dug almost painfully into my back.

"Daddy," I whimpered as he withdrew and I stared down under heavy-lidded eyes. "The door is locked."

"We're not fucking on my desk. Now that I have you, I'm gonna make sure to take my time. Something we didn't have before."

"Why did I have to get a gentleman Daddy?"

"Don't get used to it. You're going to get brutally fucked plenty."

I whined as I tried to tighten my arms around him and bring him back to where I needed him. Part of the old me that still existed felt a bit of fear at his promise to fuck me. Although through the spankings I'd earned, I'd always felt cleansed afterward. The pain he inflicted was about correction and not abuse. He'd never touched me in anger, only disappointment. He evaded my attempt to make him kiss me again. He just chuckled and leaned to the side, pulling out his wallet.

"Here's money to get something for dinner. You'll find the keys for your car—"

"My car?"

"You're going to need a safe ride to get around." The look he gave me stopped all my protests.

I didn't argue anyway because I knew it wouldn't get me anywhere. Happiness filled me at knowing he'd prepared for me to come back to him. He'd wanted me there even after the month of separation. My Daddy had waited for me.

I took the several twenties he handed me, then the house key he worked off his keyring and shoved them into my pocket. I had money. Arianna gave everyone who left some startup cash until they could get settled.

"The fridge and cabinets are pretty empty. I've been living on a lot of take-out."

"I'll make a list before I go to the store."

He cupped my cheek and stroked the calloused pad of his thumb across my bottom lip. The scar there had faded some, but the thick tissue was still raised. I'd accepted my flaws, embraced the ridges of flesh as proof I'd survived. He'd shown me that my naturally thin frame and scars weren't ugly, but it wasn't until I'd spent time away from him that I'd found myself seeing them for myself in a different light.

It hadn't been easy, and I hadn't fully accepted my body, but I was getting there. He'd helped start the healing process; I knew the rest was up to me to finish.

"Where did you go?"

"There's been so many changes. And I know you helped me with that, but I was mentally reminding myself that I had to finish healing for me."

"You do, but you know I'll be here."

"I do. Okay, I'm going to take care of your orders, and I'll have dinner ready when you get home. Two hours, right?"

"Should be. Give Daddy a kiss before you leave."

I started to lean forward, but he stood, and he gripped my hips to tug my ass to the edge of the desk. His hands slipped beneath my t-shirt, and I tensed at the rough perfection of his fingers and palms on my skin after too long. When his mouth finally touched mine, I forgot to breathe—to think. He could control me with nothing more than a kiss. I couldn't wait until we were alone at his house with nothing between us and no one to interrupt. It felt as if I'd waited a lifetime to finally come home.

TWENTY-NINE

YURI

I GROWLED as I drove my SUV into the left side of the two-car garage. I'd left West at the office to take care of the stuff I needed to, but a few hours had turned into four. My boy's sudden appearance had distracted me so badly that I'd forgotten to get his number. I hit the remote button to close the door and got out of my vehicle. My boy didn't understand how hard it was to control myself when he'd shown up at the office. I'd kept wondering when he'd come back, not if. He needed me as much as I needed him.

While I wanted to give him all the time he needed, that didn't mean I hadn't kept tabs on him with Arianna or that I hadn't threatened her to get the location of the safehouse. My feelings for him went way past want—it was a craving—an addiction. I hadn't realized how bad it was until I'd left him with Arianna. It was as if I'd left a piece of myself behind. I should've questioned my sanity in wanting to claim my boy. A boy I'd only known a matter of a month.

In that time, we'd been forced into close proximity. Our lives depended on each other. My feelings hadn't changed, but I'd set him free to clear his head to think about his own needs.

I exited the garage into the backyard that needed some major work, but I'd gotten a good deal on the house since it needed to be fixed up. When I'd sent him to the house, I was hoping he'd like it. If it was up to me, he'd spend a lot of time there whether that was in my bed or not. I was willing to go at whatever speed he needed, and if that meant roommates for a while, then that's what we'd do.

Music hit me as I approached the screen door and found the interior one open. I peeked through the mesh to find my boy moving around the kitchen. His back to me as he was cutting up vegetables and moving to the rhythm. Damn, I already liked coming home to him. Luckily, I'd sprayed the hinges, and they didn't make a sound as I eased the door open and then closed it behind me.

I hung my backpack from one of the kitchen chairs and sneaked up behind him. I grabbed him and loudly laughed as he screamed.

"Yuri," he yelled. "You scared the hell out of me. You're late."

"Seems you are too."

"I spent two hours at the grocery store. You weren't joking when you said you didn't have anything. But I unpacked my things first and made room in your dresser for them."

"Good, I would've probably made you move them when I got home anyway."

"I tried out the guest room bed, and I liked yours better."

"Brat."

"Again, all your fau—"

I cupped his cock through the soft cotton of my pajama bottoms he wore. "Did you prep for me, baby boy?"

"Yes, Daddy."

The knife he was using hit the cutting board as I kicked his bare feet apart and reached deeper between his thighs to find the hard base of his plug. My dick went instantly hard remembering the heat and tightness of him strangling the girth of my length. I made a quick check to find that the oven and stove weren't on, then I spun him and picked him up. His long, slim legs locked around my waist.

I slammed my mouth onto his. Josh's lips immediately parted, and his tongue tentatively teased mine. I easily carried him through the house and upstairs to the bedroom. After I gently laid him on our bed, I straightened and started to remove my clothes. He worked his off at the same time, and I groaned at the sight of his pale, slim form stretching. His thighs parted to expose the base of the plug.

"Stroke yourself," I ordered as I kicked my jeans aside and then opened the nightstand for a condom and lube. I tossed the items on the bed. I promised myself that I'd take my time. Our first time was about comfort and knowing the other was okay, this one I needed him to know that I wanted him for him. Just us with no outside forces threatening to come between us.

I lay beside him, then I lowered my mouth to his, and he panted as he stroked his slim length.

"Did you think of me while you were away?"

He nodded as a shiver worked along his frame.

"Good, because I jerked off thinking about fucking you again. Loving on you."

His cheeks were stained pink, and just as he froze, I grabbed his wrist and pulled his hand away from his cock.

"Daddy, please."

"Not until I say so, boy. So beautiful. Mine."

I loved on him with my lips and hands, slipped between his legs as my hands circled his wrists. I secured them in one. I didn't give him my weight. He twisted his body, trying to rub against me. I sharply nipped at his bottom lip.

"Do I need to tie you down, baby boy?"

"N-no."

"No what?"

"No, Daddy, I'll be good."

If it was torturous for him, it was even harder on me. I teased the small circles of his nipples. Bit and sucked until he was gasping and trying to get away. Sweat tickled along the valley of my spine, and my cock kept brushing my hairy thighs. I was so close to getting off it was embarrassing. But finally having him in my bed was more than I'd hoped for.

"Keep your hands on the pillow. If you disobey me, I'll spank you and put you in the corner, am I understood?"

"Yes...Daddy."

I licked along the crease of his thigh where it met his groin. He was waxed smooth. I loved the contrasts between our bodies, heavy to slim, hairy to smooth. I nuzzled his sac and started fucking him gently with the toy. Just enough to tease, I watched the way the rim of his hole flexed around the thickest part easily, and as I let the base go, it sunk back inside.

"I was going to be good, baby boy, but we have time later." I straightened to sit back on my heels, tore open the condom wrapper, and quickly sheathed my length. Just the stroke of my fingers was almost too much. I jerked the plug from him without care, then slicked his hole and my cock.

He pulled his legs back and held them in place with his arms as he pulled his cheeks apart. I slid two fingers inside to spread the lube, making sure he was ready.

"Fuck, Daddy."

I jerked my fingers from him and spanked his bottom until it was red. "Daddy doesn't like such words coming from my baby boy."

I squeezed the abused, subtle curves then lifted him to rest on my thighs. I pressed the head of my cock to his prepped entrance, and I eased forward, giving it to him inch by inch. I went deeper with every nudge of my hips.

"I want it all, please."

"You know what you're asking for?"

"You'd never hurt me."

The confidence in his gaze—the trust was too much. He'd come back to me without doubts in us. I'd succeeded in my goals of him accepting the care he should demand.

I pulled out and flipped him onto his knees, manhandled him until he was right where I wanted him. I shoved inside him with my full strength, and his head flew back as his body arched, pushing his ass higher. I grabbed his hips, and I used him, plowed his hole. Watched the rim drag along my cock. He squeezed on every retreat to try to keep me inside.

I clenched my teeth and wished for strength as I stroked my hands from his hips, over the new softness of his belly that was no longer concaved, and his nipples, scraping my nails over them. Blanketing his body with mine, I arched my hips, taking him in deep strokes until he was bracing his hands on the headboard. I pressed my mouth to his ear.

"You want it harder, don't you, baby boy?"

"Yes, hurt me, please."

"You want Daddy to own you?"

"Yes," he screamed, as I doubled my pace until the sounds of grunts and sweaty skin meeting filled the room. I bit at his neck and shoulder, sucked a mark on his shoulder blade, then went back to his ear. Licking along the curve.

I was losing control. I marked him with my ownership. His ass was tight and getting tighter as he got closer to the edge. My muscles screamed, and blood roared in my ears, so I quickly grabbed his cock, slicked it with his precum and jacked him in a brutal rhythm that matched my thrust.

A low, agonized groan filled my head as his release covered my hand and his grip on my cock intensified, and I stroked him until I shouted. I spilled into the barrier between us and ground against his ass, prolonging our pleasure until we fell to our sides. His gasp met my groan as I slipped free, and I pulled him tighter to my chest. He turned his head, and his eyes were closed as he searched for my mouth.

We lazily kissed until our bodies calmed and I pulled the covers over us as the room turned chilly. We were going to have to get up—my boy needed to be tended to and then fed. He wiggled his ass against my half-hard dick, and I shoved my hand between his thighs to circle his swollen hole.

"Did Daddy make you feel good?"

"Yes. I've only ever gotten off with you or the rare occasion I jerked off. Which I've done a lot since the last time I saw you." His voice was soft and sleepy.

"Your pleasure should always come first unless you've been bad, then Daddy will leave you unsatisfied until you learn your lesson."

"Are you really going to keep me?"

"Yes, for however long you want to stay. This is just the beginning. We have a lot to work through, but until we're sure this is forever, I'm going to own you in whatever way you allow."

"I can live with that."

I smiled as Josh completely relaxed and cuddled my arm to his chest that I had under his head. I kept playing with his hole until I forced us both to get up. He was there, and I was keeping him. We had plenty of time to spend in bed or on whatever surface I wanted to take him on.

EPILOGUE

JOSH

MUSIC VIBRATED the floor beneath my feet as I walked into Vices after coming back from running errands. I didn't know how Yuri worked in the chaos of strippers and dance music, but somehow this was his place to think. I leaned onto the bar and smiled at the regular afternoon bartender. She came over and mirrored my pose. I liked the woman who was only a few years older than me. She was working her way through college by slinging booze five afternoons a week and being the main act on Saturdays.

"Hey, Kiki, is Daddy around?"

I giggled at her epic eye roll as she nodded toward the end of the bar. I'd discovered quite a few friends over the last six months of working for my Daddy taking care of the office. I still wasn't a fan of West, but I dealt with him for the short time he spent in the office. Mainly he just picked up a job and was gone again.

"New girl has him cornered at the end of the bar. I swear that bitch is like a shark with blood in the water. She's just not getting that the man she's hoping to trap already belongs to someone else."

"Aw hell naw." I put on a thick southern accent and pushed away from the neon trimmed bar.

"Go get her, tiger."

I barely heard her above the music. A tall, slender woman in barely-there shorts and a top that was pretty much pasties with strings attached was standing there. Although, I'd kill for the heels she wore. Daddy did enjoy the occasional lap dance from his baby boy.

Jealousy was rare for me; I was confident that he only wanted me in his bed, and he'd quickly slid a ring on my finger that showed he owned me. And I hadn't protested. Actually, Daddy hadn't put it on fast enough. We hadn't done the whole official vows thing. We revisited the issue every few months. Yet, we didn't see it as a requirement. We'd spoken our own—both signed a contract that outlined our rules of conduct and expectations. Traditional marriage wasn't on it.

I'd learned that for me jealousy was a trust issue and I had all the faith in him. Not only was one of my rules to always be honest with him, but we'd promised that we'd never keep secrets.

While it bothered me someone else thought they could rub on my man, I also knew that he was all mine. Also, I had to understand he liked to work at the bar of a strip club. It was a given he'd be offered a dance or two, maybe more. I came up behind him, wrapped my arms around his waist, and laid my cheek on his cotton-covered back. I grinned at the woman's huff as Daddy patted my thigh and I cuddled closer.

"Hey, baby boy, did you get your errands done?"

"Yes, Daddy."

He took my hand and tugged me to his side, pushing the woman out of the way. I could practically hear the death tap of her heels as she stormed off. Kiki placed an espresso cup on a saucer on the bar next to his pint. I'd talked Ramone into buying an espresso machine for me. Promised I'd buy them as long as I didn't have to make them.

At this distance from the stage, the music wasn't as loud, and I looked at the files spread out in front of him.

"Being productive?"

"Not now that you're here."

"Wasn't enjoying the attention?"

A shiver worked through my body when he pinched my chin and his gaze locked with mine.

"There is only one sexy person I want dancing for me, and she wasn't it."

I knew my grin was just past goofy at knowing I was his sole focus. And his attentions had become even more intense over the months. He never failed to make sure I knew he was mine as much as I belonged to him.

"Better not be. I worked my skinny ass off to trap you."

"This ass ain't skinny."

I snorted out a laugh as he grabbed a handful of my plumper ass. I think every gram of fat ended up on my backside. My Daddy wasn't complaining, especially when it came to my spankings that had nothing to do with punishment.

"You saying I'm fat?"

He spanked my ass and knew I earned more than that when he got me home. I had a tendency to take my bratty attitude to the next level just to see how far I could push him.

"Baby boy, skinny, fat, or whatever, you're mine. You ready to go home?"

"No public spanking then?"

"No, you asked for a spanking that means corner time."

I groaned at my plan being messed up. But I wouldn't have my Daddy any other way. He knew what I needed and when. I'd spent my entire life existing as a thing to be used. An object to be shown off like a prized possession. Love was always an empty word, a prettily wrapped currency you sell your soul for. I'd learned the hard way that being cared for and cherished was worth more than someone whispering those three coveted words.

"Hey, baby boy, tell Daddy what's wrong?"

"Thank you."

"For what?"

"For caring."

"I'll always care, baby. And when the other word means more, I'll tell you that one too."

"I'd prefer if you showed me."

"Then let me get you home. Daddy's ready for some alone time with his boy."

COMING SOON

As the Blood Reigns
A Yuri Sorenson Mystery #2

Nothing ever unsettled P.I. Yuri Sorenson. As a former federal agent, he'd thought he'd seen it all. That was until a new client sashayed into his office and asked him to find her missing husband. Missing person cases weren't usually his thing, but when he learned it was her fourth husband to disappear, his curiosity took over.

He didn't know if he was searching for a body or just a wealthy man trying to escape a marriage he didn't want. When his search took him from underground BDSM clubs to the echelon of the city's high society, he didn't know who to trust or believe.

Finding out the truth wouldn't be as easy as he'd first thought and wondered if the consequences were worth the risk to his most prized possession—his husband?

ABOUT THE AUTHOR

J.M. Dabney is a multi-genre author who writes Body Positive/Diverse Romance and Fiction. They live with a constant diverse cast of characters in their head. No matter their size, shape, race, etc. J.M. lives for one purpose alone, and that's to make sure they do them justice and give them the happily ever after they deserve. J.M. is dysfunction at its finest and they makes sure their characters are a beautiful kaleidoscope of crazy. There is nothing more they want from telling their stories than to show that no matter the package the characters come in or the damage their pasts have done, that love is love. That normal is never normal and sometimes the so-called broken can still be amazing.

The author is Gender Nonconforming are uses the preferred pronouns They/Them.

ALSO BY J.M. DABNEY

Sappho's Kiss Series

When All Else Fails

More Than What They See

Dysfunction it its Finest Series

Club Revenge

Soul Collector Prophecy

Twirled World Ink Series

Berzerker

Trouble

Scary

Lucky

Brawlers Series

Crave

Psycho

Bull

Hunter

Executioners Series

Ghost

Joker

King

Sin & Saint

Trenton Security

Livingston

Little

Gage

Pure

Masiello Brothers

The Taming of Violet

3 Moments Trilogy

A Matter of Time

The Men of Canter Handyman

Black Leather & Knuckle Tattoos

Chance at the Impossible

Bloody Knuckles Bar & Grill

Clipping the Gargoyle's Wings

New West City Universe

Co-written with Davidson King

The Hunt

Standalone

By Way of Pain (Criminal Delights - Assassins)

Waited So Long

A Yuri Sorenson Mystery

Not Another Statistic